Edited by Do

ARACHOFRIGHT
Scary Spider/Insect Stories

GRAVESTONE PRESS

TABLE OF CONTENTS

Webs

Rie Sheridan Rose

There's a spiderweb in the corner—
iridescent strands of silk woven
into a complex castle
where the widow is a queen.

She captures the unsuspecting,
there in its barely visible threads,
and spins for them shrouds
fine as courtly robes.

She sips their blood like wine,
living on their death.

So I shall build my own web…
of painted rooms and trendy furnishings.
A well-stocked bar and a widescreen TV.
Calling my own captives.

I will feed them well to keep them fat.
Give them hope to share my bed.
Make them feel like kings
and emperors…

Then sink my fangs in throbbing throats
and taste my own blood wine.

Spider's Touch

Diane Arrelle

SMACK!

Glenn wasn't sure what annoyed him more, the bothersome stings from the mosquitoes swarming around him, or the stinging smacks he kept giving himself as he killed the blood-sucking pests. He smashed another mini-marsh monster and groaned, "Lord, I hate living in the country!"

"Glennnn!"

He jumped up from the lawn chair and raced toward the sound of the hysterical female voice. "Coming, Mandy," he shouted, forgetting his frustrations for the moment. "I'm coming!"

"Glenn, help me!" he heard her scream as he dashed up the steps of their home and joined her in the bedroom.

"Wha... what... is... it?" he panted. He held his aching chest with his right hand and supported himself against the door frame with his left.

Oblivious to his obvious pain, his wife, Amanda, pointed to a medium-sized brown spider sitting on the windowsill. "Kill it!" she yelled shrilly. "Glenn, get rid of it!"

"You... made... me run all the way here because of a spider?" he asked slowly, the anger and frustration returning. "Did you forget why we moved here?"

"How can I forget why we're out here in the middle of nowhere," she snapped. "We bought this godforsaken summer retreat for your health. We spent a lot of my money for your supposed stress levels, so the least you can do is get rid of that awful creature before I have another breakdown."

"All right, Amanda," Glenn sighed and killed the spider with a bedroom slipper. *She's either the stupidest woman on earth or she's trying to do me in,* he thought. He stood next to the window looking out at the endless green nature, shuddered and turned to study the woman he had married.

I've got to be the unluckiest man in the world, he mused for the millionth time and stared at Amanda, knowing he couldn't quite figure her out. Sometimes she would cling to him like he was a life preserver. She kept two beat up rag dolls in an old cigar box in her drawer and she believed she had metamorphed into a butterfly when she had her last mental breakdown.

He shook his head and wondered, *did she pick this real estate to help me or did she do it to add to her list of late husbands?*

Now that he really thought about it, it didn't seem all that far-fetched. Stanley died of a heart attack; George died from a high blood-pressure induced stroke and here he was, husband number three, suffering from anxiety and hypertension.

Could she be a killer? Glenn shuddered at the very idea. *Could Mandy be a cold-blooded murderer?*

"Why don't you go wash those dead mosquitoes off your shirt before they stain it?" she snapped.

9

"You're always so thoughtless, always making more work for me."

He nodded and slowly left the room. He changed his shirt and noticed the huge load of dirty laundry by the washer. "Better do it," he sighed as he sorted the clothes and loaded the machine, "else I'll never hear the end of it."

Glenn waited for the clothes to cycle through, then loaded the dishwasher with the dinner dishes from the night before and the morning's breakfast cups and bowls. After changing the laundry from the washer to the dryer he went back outside and sat on the lawn chair again. He tried to ignore the insects buzzing around him by daydreaming, but all he could think about was life before Amanda.

Those were the good old days, except that he hadn't enjoyed them. He'd always been in debt and he longed to share his life with someone. Then Mandy entered the picture unexpectedly, fresh out of the asylum... out of her cocoon... and shorn of her mental wings. He took her out as a favor to her brother-in-law, a co-worker he owed money.

She was nine years older than Glenn, but that hadn't bothered him. She was very pretty, very lonely and very insecure. He had loved the way she needed him. She needed him for everything and made him feel important. She made him feel like a man. It didn't hurt that she was also very rich from her first two husbands' insurance and investments. He felt that luck was finally on his side and, in a moment of lustful insanity, they married three weeks after their first date.

Now five years later, Glenn realized that he'd made a mistake. He had depended on luck that was never there for him and he wanted out. To be totally honest, he wanted some of her money too. Actually, all of it would be nice, but he was beginning to feel that if he just got away before she killed him he'd be happy.

"Damn," he muttered. "Why couldn't she be as considerate as her first husbands and drop dead?"

He glanced toward their bedroom window and noticed several dark fuzzy looking patches up near the roof. He stared at them and was amazed as they grew larger. He got up from his seat and walked over for a closer look. Right where the wall met the overhanging eaves was a sight that made his stomach clench. He fought off the sudden chill that tickled his spine as he stared at a cluster of at least fifty daddy-longlegs.

He knew they were harmless little spiders with very long, skinny legs, but those legs made them look big... big and deadly. In fact, they could scare someone who was afraid of spiders. Scare them to death.

Glenn smiled as he watched the spiders flee the sunshine and huddle together in the shade of the overhang. He looked to the right and left and noticed other fuzzy spots. *Yep,* he thought with a surge of satisfaction, *they surely could scare someone to death.*

He went to get the ladder, feeling good for the first time since Amanda made them move out here. "Well, what the hell," he said to himself. "Even if it doesn't work, at least I'll pay her back for all these years of clinging, whining and nagging."

A few minutes later he walked into the house brushing at his shoulders and hair. He scratched the back of his neck and said, "Why don't we go for a nice romantic walk before lunch. The exercise will do us both good."

Amanda started to frown, then smiled. "A romantic walk? How sweet, just let me grab the bug spray and we'll be off."

"That's fine dear," Glenn said, surprised she didn't give him an argument about the heat and insects. She disliked rural living even more than he did and continually reminded him that they were there just for his precious health. "Take your time and don't forget your sunscreen," he reminded her.

He held out his hand to her as she approached.

She smiled again, looking years younger as her frown lines turned up at the corners of her mouth. She took his hand and they set off, strolling down the path to the lake.

After a few moments of silence, Amanda sighed and moved close to him as they walked. "You know I hate to complain constantly, but I think if we spend another five weeks in this horrible place I'll have another breakdown. The insects are driving me buggy! Listen to that awful buzzing! Cripes, I think every bug in New Jersey lives here."

They walked on in silence for a few steps when she added, "I hope you appreciate all I'm doing to keep you alive!"

Glenn was starting to feel the pangs of remorse, but she'd neatly erased them with that one sentence.

He put his arm comfortingly around her shoulder then turned his head to look at her. Then, in exaggerated jerky motion, he pulled his arms away from her and jumped back, pointed at her shoulders and sputtered, "Uh... uh..."

"What is it?" she yelled, swiping at her shoulder length hair. "Is there something on me?"

Wide-eyed, he kept grunting in horror and nodding.

"Get it off! Get it off me!"

He watched her grab at something on her neck and then look at her hand. He smiled as she stared bug-eyed at the squashed spider with long twitching legs He wore a full grin as she crumpled onto the pine-needle covered trail.

"Wow, that worked better than I hoped for," Glenn said as he went to her. "Maybe my luck is finally charging." He checked for a pulse, then picked her up and carried her home. He was feeling too high from success to be bothered by that little bit of nagging guilt.

He laid her on their bed and brushed the feel of cobwebs off his shoulders. He looked in the mirror to make sure there was nothing crawling on him then sat down beside Amanda's still form.

Gently he tickled her with a feather, running it up and down her bare arms and face, then giggled with malicious glee as Amanda twitched away from his spider kisses. Then, suddenly she woke with a start, sat up and shuddered violently.

"Oh God, I can still feel it crawling on me," she wept, rubbing her arms. "I never saw such a disgusting thing before in my life. Oh Glenn, it was a monster! I want to go home!"

Glenn hugged her. "Honey, we paid for this lovely natural retreat and besides, what about me and my condition? Tell you what, why don't you take a nice hot bath and relax?"

He filled the tub with hot water and led her into the bathroom, undressed her like a child and helped her into the bath. Then he left the room.

Two minutes later she was screaming.

He had to fight with himself not to laugh like a schoolboy. He silently counting to ten, slowly opened the bathroom door and asked, "What's wrong?"

She lay in the tub, rigid with fear and pointed to the ceiling. "Get me out of here," she whimpered. "Help me up before another one falls on me."

He gently lifted her out and carried her back to the bedroom. "Before what gets you?" he asked with concern. "What frightened you, Mandy?"

"The spiders! All the spiders on the ceiling!"

He smiled and he was sure it was a kindly smile. "Oh, of course. The spiders. Why don't I just get you a tranquillizer and call Dr. Walters in the morning?"

She stared at him wildly. "There were spiders in there! There were! I'm not having another breakdown!"

"Of course you're not, Sweetheart," Glenn said, soothing her and stroking her head. "You're as sane as you've ever been. And after you take your pill, I'll go in there and get rid of all those bad, nasty spiders."

He left her resting on the bed and went into the bathroom. He swept all the spiders from the ceiling with a broom. Then he vacuumed them up. *Maybe I'm carrying this too far*, he thought fighting off a moment of guilt. *Maybe I should stop*. He looked toward the bedroom and smiled. "No way," he muttered. Luck was too much on his side now to stop. Finally, something was going one hundred percent his way.

He felt itchy and showered to wash off the imaginary arachnids crawling on his back and legs. He knew none had escaped his Hoover, but still, he could almost feel something. In all actuality, Glenn didn't like the nasty little things any better than Amanda even though he'd read that they were harmless.

Once her pills kicked in, Amanda slept the rest of the day and through the night. When he tickled her with the feather, she'd unconsciously slap at the spot, then scratch.

As dawn broke, he emptied the last bagful of arachnids onto the bed. She was starting to stir. He sat on the rocking chair beside her and waited. He felt an adrenaline high and hated to admit how much he was enjoying his own cleverness. "This is too easy," he chuckled. "Too easy."

Amanda moaned and scratched and rolled on the sheets, thrashing at the hundreds of points of contact. Each time she killed one, Glenn would gently remove the tiny dead evidence.

Suddenly she woke and bolted upright. Her eyes shifted every which way as dozens of spiders crawled on her, covering her arms, legs and nightgown. One walked down her bangs, between her eyes and onto her nose. Staring at it cross eyed, she opened her mouth and screamed... and screamed... and screamed.

An hour later the paramedics came for her. "Get them off," she begged them. "Get them off me."

The two young men looked at each other and shrugged. "Sure, lady, just tell me what I'm supposed to get off you," one said in a soothing tone.

She rolled her eyes wildly, focusing on nothing and thrashed her head from side to side. "The spiders, get them off me!" She pulled her arms from the paramedics' grip as they tried to calm her. She slapped away their hands, she clawed at her arms and neck. "Get them off me!"

Glenn watched them load her into the ambulance and he smiled, happy for the first time in years. Luck was finally on his side.

***

A month later, Glenn brought Amanda back home. Lady Luck had been fickle and his wife had recovered all too quickly.

He sat her in the living room and stared at Amanda in angry silence. She wasn't supposed to get better. The doctors originally said it could take years for her to respond to the real world again and then poof, just like that she went and got sane.

16

Amanda smiled at him with the sweet smile she used to have back when they dated. He tried to smile back, despite his annoyance at her recovery. He had to admit that at least her shrewish personality had changed for the better. She was almost the woman he had impulsively married all those years ago.

"Glenn," she said. "I really should be angry at you for what you did, but I understand. I wasn't being a good wife. And I even learned something else. Spiders are our friends!"

Hey, maybe things will be better now, Glenn thought. *Maybe we can be happy again.* He got up, walked over to her and kissed the woman he once loved. "Welcome home, Mandy."

She kissed him back and grabbed him with an unusual show of strength to force him to the floor. Glenn felt excited, aroused. He grabbed her in return and they made love like teenagers.

Finally, when they were both spent, Amanda sat up slowly and said, "I bet nobody ever mentioned to you that when I was a butterfly I could fly, or that when I became a Voodoo witch my first husband dropped dead. No Glenn, I've never been nuts. I'm just very special."

Glenn watched her from where he lay and wondered what she was talking about. He rubbed at the love bite she had given him, wishing it didn't sting so much.

"No, Glenn, I'm not a crazy person at all, I'm just very different," Amanda explained with a girlish giggle. "I just relate to things differently. I empathize, become one with things. Like butterflies.

I always feel such guilt whenever I think about how poor George keeled over the day I showed him my beautiful wings."

Glenn frowned; he was feeling dizzy. And what was she rambling on about. Wings... husbands... He struggled to focus on her words.

"And I'll let you in on a little secret, I never loved Stanley, he beat me. I used the doll on him in self-defense. So, while I was in the hospital this time I learned to relate to spiders, I really love them now. You showed me that they really aren't harmful and in their own way they are very beautiful."

Glenn tried to sit up but couldn't.

"Pay attention," Amanda shouted at him. "Watch this!"

He tried to see what she was doing, but he just didn't have the energy. His arms felt so heavy, in fact his whole body felt leaden. He was tired. He closed his eyes. He could feel his heartbeat getting slower with each passing second.

"Glenn! Open those eyes and watch this," Amanda yelled from a distance and yet right above him.

With a great deal of effort, Glenn forced his eyes opened and stared at his wife dangling over him. She was suspended from the ceiling by a thin thread.

"See, honey?" she gushed. "I told you I could be different. I decided I liked spiders so much I wanted to be one. Did you know the black widow paralyzes her mate after sex and then eats him? Isn't that neat!"

18

Glenn wanted to yell, wanted to run, but couldn't, so he laid there and watched her descend. When she reached him, Amanda kissed his lips softly, then ripped his shirt off. Glenn tried to scream when she bared her new fangs in a happy smile.

He succeeded when she began to feed.

The Jorogumo:
a Japanese legend re-spun in haiku form

Terrance V. Mc Arthur

(Jorogumo—a legendary Japanese creature, a spider who lives and grows for 400 years. The spider receives shape-changing powers. It is able to appear as a beautiful, young woman to entice the unwary men she captures and devours.)

Jorogumo spins,
her massive web the product
of four hundred years.

Now, she gains power;
her spider skin disappears
to show a fair maid.

A samurai on
the road sees a beauteous
lady; he draws near.

She smiles at him; her
sheer kimono sparkles like
dew, tempting the man.

She flutters her fan,
inviting him to approach;
how close will he get?

He gently loosens
the sash of her silken obi
and gazes deeply.

She strikes! Venom sprays!
The samurai's sword flashes,
and her head drops off.

The warrior smiles;
he knew her monstrous nature
when first he spied 'er.

No Turning Back

Theresa Jacobs

Liam hacked aside low-hanging branches and brush, shouting, "HA! HA!" emulating the staunchest of trail blazers with a stick, imagining it was a razor-sharp machete. "I do believe there is gold in them there hills," he called, pointing towards the rocky escarpment.

"Hold up, I gotta water the plants," Jessie yelled over Liam's noise. He was shyer than his two friends, so he ducked left away from their prying eyes and possible taunts.

Cole slapped a mosquito from his face, pulled his ball cap lower to protect his ears and whinged, "Are you sure we won't get lost?"

"How?" Liam stopped and pointed up. "How can we get lost? The escarpment is right there. We live" — he turned aiming the long stick across Cole's cheek towards the crushed underbrush — "back there. You can see it out your windows, right?"

Cole nodded, stamping his feet to shake away the voracious insects gnawing at his thin pale legs.

"Yeah, but—"

"Hey, guys! I found a cave," Jessie shouted.

A grin spread across Liam's dirt smeared face. "See? Gold!" He beat them a shortcut under the canopy of trees to where Jessie waited. The self-proclaimed bravest of them, Liam barrelled in and grabbed the wall of grapevines covering a dark opening. "Awesome. It really is a cave. I wonder if there are gold mines around here? I bet there's treasure hidden, too."

"Or a dragon that's been sleeping for centuries," Jessie said, drawing an imaginary sword and swiping at the forest.

Cole grimaced. "How about a real live bear?" He shook his head. "Let's go, okay? I'm getting hungry."

"And pass this up? Naha, you can stay out here," Liam said, leaving his friends no chance for debate as he unceremoniously stepped into the hole.

Jessie stooped through the low entrance after him. Once inside, the entrance widened, allowing Jessie to move beside Liam who already had his cell phone out, flashlight on and was peering ahead. Cole stayed to the rear, pressed into their backs, and nervously inspected the rocky ceiling.

"How far do you think it goes?" Jessie asked.

"Looks like it gets taller up ahead, let's go on and find out," Liam replied.

"Uh, can we not and say we did?" Cole said under his breath, knowing they weren't going to listen to him. But he wasn't going to stay behind alone to be ridiculed for the rest of his life. While his friends walked on, pondering their fantasies of lost treasure, he watched the ceiling for fissures and seemed to be the only one who noticed the temperature rising rather than falling. He looked back. "Guys?" he said and bumped into Jessie as they stopped without warning.

"It's a branch off to another tunnel," Liam said, ignoring Cole. "Split up?"

Cole tried again. "Guys, I can't see the entrance anymore. We should go back."

Jessie brought his own phone up and flashed it around. "Maybe Cole's right. We don't know how far this'll go. So far it's boring," he finished, hoping he didn't sound scared too, even though deep down something felt off.

"Fine," Liam said, giving them false hope for a brief second. "We'll keep going straight,"

The rocky enclosure continued in its banality. Occasionally it would widen and allow them to walk three abreast, then it would narrow and squeeze them into single file. Cole wasn't sure if the rising heat was reality, or just him. The air felt humid and dense. Sweat broke out on his brow, and his pits smelt rank. It seemed as though they'd been walking forever, but a quick glance at his phone showed only forty minutes passed since he'd left home. A noise caught his breath. It sounded like his dog's nails clacking on the hardwood floor. "Hey," he called in a loud whisper.

"What's that?" Jessie said, cocking his head.

The sound echoed around the walls, indiscernible as to where it was coming from.

The meagre light from Liam's phone played out, unable to penetrate more than four feet ahead. "Is that a wall?" he asked, the disappointment at a possible end clear in his voice.

They leaned in together, peering ahead.

"Is it moving?" Jessie whispered.

Liam spoke even lower out of the corner of his mouth, "Reminds me of the predator's optical illusion camouflage."

The clacking sound grew. What first seemed to be a wall roiled and churned, somehow, impossibly, getting closer.

Movement along the walls drew their lights. Cole was the first to scream as thousands of tiny eyes reflected back at them. What they at first mistook for a wall was a mass of large, writhing insects. They overflowed the tunnel, piling into a solid mass. Some, faster than their mates, skittered across the ceiling, seeking food.

"RUN!" Liam screamed, turning into Jessie and pushing him to the ground.

Jessie knocked his head against the rocky wall. Blood spurted from the wound where a sharp outcrop had gashed him open. The coppery scent must have appealed to the creatures. A high-pitched keening echoed around them.

"Come on!" Cole cried as one of the things dropped from the ceiling onto Jessie's head. It was the size of a mouse and unlike anything Cole had seen in his life. It was dusty white, with thick pincers similar to those of an ant, except it had eight clear, shiny eyes across the top of its face and too many legs to stop and count. Its jaw opened behind the pincers, revealing a row of razor-sharp teeth and it let out a 'nails on chalk board' screech.

In the split second all this registered, Cole flung his phone at the thing, knocking it off his friend and pulled Jessie up at the same time.

They ran as the hungry throng kept coming. Jessie stumbled, his head injury causing dizziness. Cole held him up. Liam's light faded from sight, leaving them to get out on their own. "I can't believe he left us," Jessie sobbed. "If we get out of this, he's not my friend anymore."

"Shush," Cole said—not because he cared about Liam the trouble maker—but because they needed their air to keep running. His mind went to Jessie's words. *If we get out...* and he thought back to the hour before and how quickly life could change. His ifs were, if only he hadn't answered Liam's text. If only he hadn't agreed to wander behind their houses where they weren't allowed. If only his mother said, *no you can't play with your friends today.*

He ran for his life, longing to be back to that hour before this hell, where he sat on the faux suede sofa, eating soggy cereal. His annoying older brother, Jim, giving knuckles to his scalp while his mom yakked away on the phone. At the moment he hated his life. Hated his brother and worse, hated the sound of his mother's voice. Now he'd give anything to be there with his family, where he was safe and cosy.

"I see light," Jessie said, batting at one of the bugs as it tumbled down the wall beside him. It ricocheted off the wall, hit Cole's knee with a dull thud and screamed as they left it behind. They both desperately wanted to see how close the beasts were, but neither dared pause to attempt it.

The light was growing and the air was cooling. Their hearts soared. The light winked out and Cole gasped, about to cry *What now*? when Liam reappeared twenty feet ahead at the tunnel exit.

"Hurry! Come on!" he shouted, waving them forward.

If they had any air left in their lungs, they would have yelled back, *"What do you think we're doing*!" But they couldn't and they pushed forward harder still. Cole shoved Jessie into the narrower exit and shot out of the tunnel right behind him. Without the hard rock floor beneath their feet, they tangled into the brush and tree roots and fell in a pile.

"W-h-a-t," Cole huffed, unable to speak and catch his breath, but knowing they needed to keep running. He climbed off Jessie to see what Liam was planning and to see if the things were still coming. He gaped at the sight. While they'd been running, Liam had exited the tunnel and found the biggest dead brush he could. Now he was attempting to shove it in the opening.

Jessie climbed to his feet, shouting, "Let's go!"

"Wait," Liam cried. "They're close, help me!"

Jessie was about to turn and run home when Cole grabbed his arm. He looked and finally understood. Liam had set the bush on fire and was pushing it back into the hole. They grabbed the thick arm of the branch and helped Liam cram it through the gap.

Smoke billowed out of the mouth like an old chimney. The black soot stained the escarpment wall. The insects shrieked and squealed in ear splitting agony. When not one of them seemed to

27

have passed Liam's barrier, Cole said, "Please, let's go home now."

Even though Liam had left them at first, he had stayed for the most important part and the three boys walked home together, forever changed from who they were the hour before.

Welcome To My Parlour

Tom Leaf

It was five-thirty on a Wednesday evening when Edward, seven years old and small for his age, wandered into the kitchen.

'There's something waiting in my room.' The statement was made without drama.

'That's nice, dear,' his mother replied, poised in the act of slicing an onion. Beside her, a pan sat patiently waiting to be filled with water. Or gravy. Or something similar.

'Supper won't be long, so do run upstairs and wash your hands. Perhaps you could lay the table for me, too?'

This was not an unreasonable request and, on any other day, the boy would have immediately obliged.

'I don't think you heard me, Mummy. I said, there's something waiting in my room.' Edward repeated, his tone a little peevish.

'Hands, please. And the nice napkins. After all, tonight's supper is a special one, remember?'

The boy paused. 'I'm not fibbing, Mummy. There really is something waiting in my room and I don't want it to stay there.'

His mother turned, wiping her hands on her apron and, for a brief pause, she held his gaze.

'Very well, Edward. I'm listening. Who's hiding in your room?'

'Not who, what.' he corrected. 'Not a person like you or me. Something else.'

'Well, I don't see how. No-one else is in the house apart from you and me. Besides, besides, your bedroom is so full up with toys and books and other lovely things, I really can't see how there would be room enough for someone, sorry, something else.'

His mother turned back to the onion. The matter was, apparently, closed.

'Edward, dear?' Mummy's voice was a little firmer now. 'Cleanliness is next to Godliness. Hands, please.'

The bathroom at the top of the stairs was neat and clean, but always cold. Even though he couldn't see himself in the mirror--probably because he was too short--Edward knew that his thin, black hair would be firmly in place.

He sniffed his hands. They smelt clean to him and so he allowed himself to forgo any interaction with the swollen bar of soap that squatted in the porcelain dish next to the sink.

Back downstairs, Edward noticed that the table had already been laid with the nice napkins and all necessary items of cutlery were neatly in place. He supposed that had been something Mummy had done whilst he had been upstairs. Upstairs, not washing his hands.

'The table looks lovely, Edward.' Mummy said. 'Such a good boy. Thank you.'

Edward pursed his lips in confusion. 'Mummy?'

'Yes, Edward, dear.' his mother replied.

'My room. Please can we take a look in my room before supper?'

'Patience is a virtue, Edward. Do you remember when Daddy taught you that?'

'Yes, I do remember.' Edward paused. 'Is Daddy having supper with us tonight, Mummy?'

'Oh, I expect so, dear. Though he has been a little distant of late.'

Edward and his mother stood quite still, waiting for the other to speak. The onion remained unsliced. Some minutes passed and, as if in indication of this, the heavy oak clock quietly loitering within a shadowy corner of the kitchen, ticked back and forth.

'So, Mummy. My room? Please will you take a look with me?'

'Very well, worry-wart.' his mother replied softly. 'Take my hand.'

They took the stairs, mother and son, in slow parade.

At the top, just past the chill bathroom they turned to face Edward's room, just ahead of them at the end of a short, neat corridor.

'Let's go now, you and I, and see what all the fuss is about.' Mummy whispered.

Edward glanced down at his shiny shoes. He could see his worried face reflected back at him.

'See how soft our carpet is, Edward,' Mummy continued, 'our footsteps are so quiet that we certainly won't disturb whatever is waiting for us in your room.'

Edward stopped.

'Mummy. Please don't say words like that. You're scaring me.'

Mummy smiled, perhaps in an attempt to ease his fear, but the sheer width of her smile caused Edward some concern.

'You're a big scaredy-boo. Come now, Edward, there's nothing in that room that we haven't seen before. Is there?'

Mummy's thin, cool hand still held firmly onto Edward's and so, in this way, they continued their soft, soundless creep towards his bedroom. Mother and son paused in the doorway. The room before them was a testament to Edward's tidy nature. A place for everything and everything in its place.

As Daddy once said.

Books and toys were neatly stacked exactly where they were supposed to be.

'There you are, you big silly.' cooed Mummy, her smile now stretching thinly from ear to ear. 'Everything is fine. Nothing wrong here.'

'You're hurting my hand,' Edward protested, wriggling his four fingers in an attempt to break free.

'Shush now, child.' Mummy crooned. 'Look.'

In the furthest corner of the room, thick with shadows, a mass of knotted webs swiftly spidered their way up from behind Edward's wardrobe, skittering across the wallpaper from both sides and creeping upwards towards the ceiling.

'Remember, Edward, we mustn't make quick, loud noises. Daddy doesn't like those.'

At this, the room flexed and the dwindling daylight that still seeped through the veiled windows flickered and spat in protest. Edward's wardrobe bulged and cracked in an attempt to contain whatever mewling abomination hammered and roared in hungry anticipation.

'Spare the rod and spoil the child.' hissed Mummy, her face now fully split width ways, her smile infinitely stacked with small, sharp teeth.

'Please, Mummy. I don't want to see. Please can we have supper like we planned?'

For a child of seven, his stoicism in the face of the unfolding horror was admirable.

'Look, Edward,' Mummy sang, 'Daddy's here. It is so important that families eat together.'

'No, Mummy. Please.'

'Don't trouble yourself, Edward.' chuckled Mummy, her voice thick with threat. 'Supper is now most definitely served.'

Hairs On The Back Of The Neck

Dorothy Davies

"It's not an unusual phobia, Mr Tomlinson. Many people are afraid of spiders." The hypnotherapist was calmness personified, as he should be, thought Harry. But he had no idea...

"It's not just spiders ... well; I suppose it is, really."

"We can treat this. Would you like to make an appointment? I'm sorry my receptionist isn't here today, if you could give her a call tomorrow..."

"I will; thank you."

Harry put the phone down and cursed. Why couldn't he just tell the man the truth? No, it wasn't an unusual phobia but the situation he was in and that –

Could he just up and tell someone?

No.

"It's not like my house is dirty," he told his neighbour over the fence, a bit shamefaced but wanting to tell someone, "but I just found a jar of peanut butter in the fridge-"

"Not a good idea, Harry." Old Tam interrupted, always had done. "It won't spread."

"I know, I went to put it in the cupboard and do you know? Its death date was two years ago!"

"Still be all right, though."

"Maybe, wasn't going to risk it, though."

34

"You had any more trouble with spiders, Harry? Remember one time when you said you had a giant one in there."

"Well, sometimes, comes and goes, you know."

"Don't like them much myself, but you know what they say, if you want to live and thrive – let a spider run alive."

"I do that, Tam, I do that. Can't bear to kill anything."

Especially the one I have in the house, he thought, but said nothing about it.

Someone else he couldn't tell.

Next port of call, the local authority.

"Is there anyone in the Pest Control department who knows about getting rid of spiders?"

"Not really, sir, do you have much of a problem?"

"Well, there's one very large one..."

"We wouldn't send someone out for one, sir. Sorry."

But this one is... no, they would call the people in white coats if he told them.

"Thanks anyway."

They'd be sorry one day that they didn't listen.

Harry went back into his lounge and stared at the spider which had all eight legs curled up under its huge body and took up the entire sofa.

"I just want my house back," he told it. "That's all. And no one wants to help me."

The spider reached out a long lazy leg and gently tickled the hairs on the back of Harry's neck.

"All right," he sighed. "You can stay."

35

By Invitation Only

Edward Ahern

"I'm going to die pretty soon."

Dora paused in rolling the husk across the kitchen floor. "Mother, you've been saying that for decades."

"No, my mother told me what to watch for. I'm dried up now, can't inject, can't spin. I can't even digest the juice you provide. I know you don't want to talk about it, Laseodora, but I want you to have children while I'm still around."

Dora sighed and resumed pushing the silk wrapped oblong ball toward the back garden. Even drained and desiccated, it was forty pounds of bones and skin, more than she felt like toting. She spoke over her shoulder.

"Mother, we've already chewed this into stupor. I'm not excited about thirty or forty little ones scrabbling around the house. And the thought of having a man inside me is detestable." She shuddered and her four vestigial limbs jiggled on her ribs.

She trundled the husk down the back stairs and rolled it into the plowed vegetable garden patch near the mulberry trees. The earth was loose and she quickly shoveled out a resting place for her last date. Their landscaper, Vespis, had been instructed not to disturb the garden soil.

When she came back in her mother was still grumbling. "Does she listen to Theraposa? Of course not. We must breed - she must breed."

Dora picked up a half finished sweater and resumed knitting. Her mother, still, muttering, knitted a scarf. Their hand movements were sure and deft, the finished material jumping out from their needles

Thera and Dora paid their bills by selling knitted goods at craft fairs every weekend, augmented by the cash Dora was able to retrieve from her dates. Word of mouth recommendations kept their stall busy.

Thera resumed her nagging. "Dora, there are few enough of us and getting fewer. Most of the women I knew when I was your age died without issue. You can't leave this world to the humans! Suck in your repugnance and give me grandchildren."

"Mother, you know how gruesome it is for me to be pleasant with a man for the three or four hours it takes to bring him here. How much I hate their pawing and slobbering." Dora's pincers snapped forward from the back of her mouth at the thought.

"What about Vespis? His scent is less offensive than most and he seems easy to intimidate."

"He does seem nicer than most, but really, our gardener, mother? Besides he's known to come here regularly."

"Okay, let it go. But Dora, for Arachne's sake, if you love me, create new life for us before I have to leave you. You must feed soon, choose carefully next time and use him thoroughly before you put him to sleep."

There was nothing more to say. The two women knitted into the dusk and parted to sleep with only a few more words.

Three days later, Dora had to go out and gather dinner. She sniffed carefully at the man across from her in the bar. No odor of burnt tobacco or cocaine, just scent rot from the man's sweaty armpits. He sprouted coarse hair everywhere, but then so did Dora, who had to shave her bristles closely before she went out. She tried not to twitch when his hand grasped her thigh.

"The drinks are cheaper back at my place."

"What did you say your name was?"

"Ephie."

"Ephie, that's an odd name for a pretty woman."

"It's short for an even odder name, Ephebopus."

"All right, Ephie, let's go."

She led the man into her bedroom - not her lair, not where she slept, but a killing chamber with a double bed. He was sloppy drunk and fumbling out of his clothes when Dora grabbed him from behind and inhaled deeply, sucking in the reeks of booze and a badly wiped ass and lust hormones. *I can't,* she screamed to herself, *I can't!*

Dora jumped on his back, wrapped long legs around his belly fat and jabbed him with the barb on her extended coccyx. She clung as he thrashed, crooning a very human lullaby - "Go to sleep, go to sleep, close your sweet little eyes..."

The next afternoon the two pear shaped women sat without speaking, knitting needles whirling. Thera had been able to suck in only a little of the body juices Dora provided. Her torso was flabby from involuntary starvation.

"I can't move without falling, Dora, you'll have to help me get around."

"Okay, Mother. I did try, I really did. I just couldn't open myself up to him."

Thera stared back with rheumy eyes. "I know you couldn't, sweetie. We're going to have to take a chance. When Vespis shows up later this week ask him to come in to see me."

"Vespis is just another man, Mother, almost as detestable as the others."

"Familiarity doesn't just breed contempt, Dora, it also fosters acceptance. Let's see what we can do."

Dora went out to where Vespis was pruning branches. His long arms waved like an orchestra conductor as he snipped. His wide mouth split into a smile when he saw her.

"It's so good to see you again, Miss Dora. What can I do for you?"

Dora studied him. His angularity was almost pleasing, his constant attention to her flattering. "My Mother wants to speak with you, Vespis, please come in."

Dora escorted him into the parlor. He smelled of raw earth and fresh sweat, but his mammal funk was mild, more acidulous, more like Thera and Dora. Dora backed up and left Vespis standing in front of Thera.

Thera stared at him. Tall and narrow waisted, legs and arms bent at acute angles. She sniffed, then nodded to Dora, signaling satisfaction with his aroma.

"Vespis, how long have you been working for us?"

He was a quiet man and rarely spoke except with Dora. "Six months, Mrs. Octalus."

"Long enough that we should get to know each other better. Are you married?"

"No ma'am, I live alone."

"Family here in Abbotsville?"

"I arrived here about the time I started working for you. My family is pretty well dispersed and we don't keep in contact."

"That's too bad. Family is everything. Are you busy this week? I may have a special project I'd like you to work on. Could you come by tomorrow evening, after dark?"

Vespis smiled widely without showing his teeth. "Yes ma'am, glad to. I was hoping to work more with you and Dora."

Dora showed him into the parlor the next night and stayed in the room. Thera smiled at him. "Sit down, Vespis."

He bent stiffly into the chair and looked at Thera with happy expectation, an expression that changed only slightly when Dora hit him, then dragged him into the killing room where she shackled him around the neck with a steel cable that

40

ended at the radiator. When he woke up he was lying on the double bed, shoes off and pockets emptied.

Dora was sitting across the room.

"Vespis, this isn't personal."

"Miss Dora, let me go, I won't say anything." But he sounded half-hearted, as if he didn't really mean it.

"Would you be willing to have sex with me?"

"Ma'am?"

"Not right now. Think about it. Take your time. Your wire's long enough so you can reach the bathroom. I'll feed you and every night I'll lie next to you for an hour or so, until I'm ready. I'm a lot stronger than you are and if you try anything, I'll hurt you badly."

"Ma'am, Dora, I guess I have to do what you tell me, but I think it'll end badly."

"We're going to start now."

Dora laid down next to Vespis. She breathed in his aroma and was surprised that there was no stink of fear, just a refreshing, half-sour musk. She got up a half hour later, still without touching him, and left.

She fed him twice a day and changed his sheets every two days. One of Vespis' other customers called to complain he had not shown up at their house and asked if Thera and Dora had seen him. Dora sympathized, but told them that Vespis was a vagrant and probably taken off.

Dora used her mother's bedroom for feeding purposes. Like Dora, her mother had a separate lair and Dora half carried Thera in and out of it each

41

day. Thera had switched from complaining to pep talks about the wonders of child birth.

Dora gradually began to touch Vespis' face and genitals and allowed Vespis to do the same to her. Her breasts were meaningless and Vespis seemed to sense this, for he stroked her arms, face and private parts without showing any interest in her chest.

"Vespis, It's funny but I don't hate you as much as I do other men."

"It's possibly because I'm not much like other men. I'm truly sorry for the situation we're getting into. You're not human, not really. Can I ask what you are?"

"We're a hybrid of spiders and people and need to breed with humans. It's not personal. I like you, sort of, but I need you to copulate with me."

Vespis appeared relieved, as if he had needed Dora's confirmation.

"I'm not afraid, Dora. I think we can do this."

A week of increasingly intimate comfort passed quickly. One morning, after preparing another comatose date for feeding, Dora entered her bedroom wearing only a long sleeved blouse and sweater.

"Vespis, I want to try and couple."

"I think I've been ready since the first night."

Dora pulled off his trousers. She laid back down on the bed, careful to keep her coccyx stinger retracted. He mounted her without foreplay. Dora sensed a pleasant chemical heat, almost mentholated, and cuddlingly warm. It was over in a few moments but Dora wasn't disappointed. She resisted the urge to kill him and left, bringing her mother liquid from the last night's sting.

Thera couldn't drink, but beamed on seeing her. "You've actually done it! You didn't kill him, did you? Remember that you need to do it several more times to ensure you're gravid."

"No, Mother. It was surprisingly pleasant, not human nasty. Vespis is almost too perfect."

Dora and Vespis mated twice daily for another week. Small stirrings began within her and Dora knew that her clutch of perhaps a hundred eggs had been fertilized. She came to him that night for the last time.

Vespis sensed the finality before she said a word. "Dora, you're much stronger than I am. Tonight, could you take off my collar so we could be together without restraint?"

Dora had a rush of almost motherly sympathy for him. "All right, Vespis, but if you run I'll have to hurt you."

The pairing was slower and more complex than before. Dora felt a burning heat and then numbness inside her. She clutched at the sides of Vespis' torso and felt little protuberances that shouldn't be there. She threw Vespis off the bed and then fell back, unable to get up.

"What's happening to me? What are you?"

Vespis sat next to her on the bed and stroked her face.

"Dora, my poor Dora. You noticed my other two appendages. And I knew about your other four. I'm so sorry, but it had to be."

Vespis touched her stomach. "You're going to be the mother of my children. But not the way you think. Your eggs will hatch into my children and not yours. My children will eat you for nourishment. I almost wish you had stung me instead."

"Why can't I move?"

"You're paralyzed dear, just as you'd have done to me. If it's a consolation I'm also dying, now that the copulation is complete."

Dora felt herself losing focus. "But what about Mother?"

"I'm afraid she'll have to die on her own. There's no pain. You'll fall asleep soon."

"But Vespis, you were with us for half a year."

"Yes, darling, and I waited to be invited into your parlor."

The Widow of Ilken Fen

David Turnbull

There's a windmill on Ilken Fen. White sails starkly contrasting the black painted wooden slats of its tower. To be more accurate, it's in fact a wind pump. Before the advent of steam and electricity such constructs littered the fens. They are slightly smaller than a traditional windmill and their pumps helped drain sections of the marshlands as part of a once burgeoning local peat industry. Today there's is a single surviving pump on Ilken, restored and renovated, protected and maintained by English Heritage.

It was out to the fens, on a route that passes the wind pump, I decided to walk one day to break the monotony of home working during the Covid lockdown. I live in Cambridgeshire so the drive to the village of Ilkendale, where my walk would begin, was not too long and, as far as I could tell, not in breach of any of the restrictions put in place at that time.

The weather forecast was for a mild but cloudy day. I had however brought waterproofs in case of an unexpected downpour. I had bottled water, a flask of coffee and some sandwiches in my backpack, along with a pair of binoculars for spotting wild birds in the wide vista of the fens. Of course I had brought sturdy walking boots, suitable

45

for the marshy underfoot conditions that would prevail on sections of my walk.

It was on the drive to Ilkendale that I began to feel suddenly overwhelmed by an inexplicable sense of impending dread. It was so intense that my pulse momentarily increased in pace. I worried that the months of Government enforced confinement might be bringing on the onset of a mild form of agoraphobia. I hadn't exactly been housebound, but this was farthest I had been from my hometown in almost a year.

More than a little unsettled, I switched on the car radio and tried to lose myself in the music, attempting also to convince myself that it was entirely natural to have a reaction of some sort after being cooped up in front of my home PC for so long. I felt sure that I would not be the first or the last to experience such an emotional reaction as we eased out of the worst of the pandemic. By the time I arrived at the small off road parking area I still felt somewhat unsettled. However, the intensity had abated considerably.

I had a map downloaded and printed off. It was a relatively easy circular walk of little more than six miles, ending up back at the start point in the village. I'd chosen it specifically for its ease and simplicity. I didn't want to risk anything too onerous on my first tentative venture back to a semblance of normality.

I was fifteen minutes or so into my walk when I realised that I hadn't seen another soul. I supposed that as it was a week day it wasn't surprising. There might have been plenty of walkers out on the fens on a weekend, even more on a public holiday, especially now restrictions were being relaxed. It didn't worry me too much. I was growing to quite like solitude.

Anne, my live in partner of three years, had moved out a month or so before the first lockdown was announced. I suppose it was a blessing in disguise. Neither of us were very accomplished in the art of compromise. I don't think we would have coped well with close, enforced proximity. In the intervening months I had discovered to my surprise that I actually quite like my own company.

Nevertheless, I was curious as to whether there was anyone at all ahead of me on the circular route, so I retrieved the binoculars from my backpack. I scanned left and right across the flatness of the landscape. I could the reeds swaying in the wind and the shafts of sunlight breaking through the clouds glinting on pools of water. There was plenty of movement from birds of different varieties: bitterns, woodcock and snipe. I saw a flock of swallows take flight and arc in synchronised unison across the sky. But I didn't discern even the slightest hint of another human being.

A couple of moorhens gliding along one of the shallow watery channels caught my attention. I zoomed the binoculars in on them. It was then I caught a glimpse of the shadow of something creeping slowly through the reeds. There seemed to a malevolence of ill intent in the manner of its movement. Once more that feeling of unease filled me.

I zoomed out a little, thinking it might be a feral cat stalking its intended prey. There was discernibly nothing there. I zoomed in again on the moorhens. They appeared unperturbed. I dismissed it as a trick of the light, or shadows of clouds passing in the sky, I slipped the binoculars back into my backpack and went on my way.

The air grew quite chilly and, when I looked up the sun, I saw the sky was being shrouded within the maelstrom of a churning black cloud. The day darkened. The echoing sounds of the bird call seemed imbued with ominous undertones. Without warning, the feeling of dread seized me again. All at once the fens seemed bleak and dismal and foreboding. The urge to turn back, get in my car and drive straight home was almost irresistible.

Had only I heeded it!

Instead, I tensed my shoulders and pushed on. This was an easy walk and the downloaded map suggested it would take an hour to an hour and a half maximum. I wasn't going to succumb to whatever post lockdown trauma was trying get it claws into me.

I began walking at a brusque pace, head slightly down, thumbs looped through the straps of my backpack. I reached a section of the path that had been gravelled for better underfoot purchase. The steady crunch of my boot heels gave a forward momentum to my pace.

I was making good headway and already I could see the outline of the wind pump in the far distance. Then to the left of me across a shimmering expense of still water, I glimpsed that creeping shadow again. This time it seemed to a rise like sooty vapour above the reed bank.

I found I was frozen to the spot as dark fronds appeared to coagulate into thick arachnid limbs which danced and writhed upwards from a huge obsidian mass, still partially concealed by the reeds. They moved with an apparent intelligent intent. Instinct told me to run but a mixture of shock and fear had me trapped to the spot. All I could do squeeze my eyes tight shut and tense myself rigid.

After a moment, when I had experienced no sensation of anything drawing close, I opened them again. The sun had broken through the clouds and whatever I'd seen, or imagined I'd seen, was gone. A coot lit down on the water and glided toward the reeds, on the hunt for insects. I rationalised that what I had witnessed was a natural phenomenon.

I was sure I'd read something somewhere about certain conditions out on the marshlands producing a form of methane gas. Your mind could summon imaginary things within a dense billow gas, just as it could within a cloud formation. Convincing myself that such a phenomenon was all that I'd experienced I pushed on, more determined than ever now that I would complete the route.

I eased myself into a steady pace again, head down, thumbs looped once again through the straps of my backpack. I could feel my heart pumping. I breathed in deep, filling my lungs with the crisp fresh air, so glad to be free of the constraints of the surgical masks we'd been obliged to wear in shops and on public transport. An energetic hike was going to be as good for me as a cardiovascular workout. My mood lifted as the blood pumping through my veins released positive endorphins.

I was steadily drawing closer to the water pump.

I could see the slow rotation of the white sails.

Unease, however, still nagged at the fringes of my thoughts. For fear of catching another glimpse of the dark swirl of shadow, I focused my attention straight ahead, specifically on the sails of the wind pump. A breeze was blowing across the fens, slowly rotating them. The motion of the blades' circuitous revolutions had a somewhat hypnotic effect on me. It reeled me in. Drawing me like a moth to a flame. My pace became more vigorous. Sweat ran down my back, warm beads trickling from my forehead over my face to drip from my chin. I was breathing heavily. The ache of the exertion set off a satisfying pulse in my calves and thighs.

This is good for you, I assured myself. Exactly why you came out here.

But, as the wind pump loomed ever larger ahead of me, I began to experience a disconcerting sensation akin to vertigo. It felt as if the path before me was inexplicably rising and dipping in erratic undulations. A foul bile rose in my throat as a debilitating nausea swept over me. I stumbled and slowed my pace, intending to rest and drink some water. But before I could come to a complete halt the ground before me seemed to judder. It had the effect of a rug being pulled from under my feet. In turn, I lurched forward and fell heavily on my knees, grazing the palms of my hands.

A new thought occurred to me as I lay there. Fracking. Maybe an energy conglomerate was conducting trials beneath the fens, blasting rock and, in the process, causing minor earth tremors. That would certainly explain the release of noxious gases that could somehow warp your senses.

The scratches on my hands from catching my fall were not too deep. I wiped off the surface blood with a tissue, then pulled myself to a seated position and fished the bottle of water from my backpack. I drank deeply. Then examined my knees. My trousers were muddy from my fall, but the material wasn't torn. I hoped that this meant the skin of my knees wasn't torn either.

I laughed out loud at my stupidity and awkwardness.

The laugh echoed and caused some of the birds to take flight.

I got slowly to my feet and noticed that I was now only a few yards away from the wind pump. Still coping with residual dizziness, I gazed up at the sails and felt like Don Quixote comically contemplating a giant. Then it hit me. So hard I was almost knocked back down again. The sense that there was something on the path behind me, looming up on me, its shadow shrouding my back in a cloak of darkness. I knew this to be the case. There was an irrefutable, blood chilling certainty to it.

To turn and confront it? Or to run? This was the dilemma I faced. What if all it turned out to be was another walker, trying to catch up on me so he or she could exchange a pleasant greeting? How pathetic I'd look if I ran from them. How rude, in that era of isolation and social distancing, to shun a possible moment of social contact with a fellow human being.

With every ounce of courage I could muster I pivoted on my heels and swung around.

I found nothing there. Just the path I'd traversed, stretching back across that flat, bleak landscape. But there was movement. The reeds to the side of the bank were swaying. The water before them shimmering with circular ripples. Had something passed through the reeds and submerged itself when it saw me stop and turn? Had that something been stalking me?

I felt trapped out there. Alone and vulnerable. The route map marked the wind pump as its half way point. Whether I turned back or carried on it would make no difference. The distance back to the village and the sanctity of my car would be the same.

I held the binoculars up to my eyes, hands trembling slightly, turning full circle and scanning for any shadowy sign of movement. All I could see here and there were clusters of varying species of waterfowl. Nothing lurking behind the reeds, slowly closing in on me. Suspicion or illusion? Hard fact or hallucination? I had no real clue what it was I was experiencing.

Somewhat unsteadily I carried on along the path until I was level with the wind pump. I could hear the creak and groan of the white sails as they rose and fell, whooshing as they ascended and sliced back down. Somehow the physicality of its presence reassured me. Here was a device devised by human ingenuity to tame and shape the wild wilderness of the fens. In the face of such intelligent technology, even as basic as this, how could I harbour superstitious notions about being stalked by some shadowy entity?

I sat down on the coarse grass before the wind pump and used my little pen knife to flick out some of the gravel that had embedded itself in the treads of my boots. Then I took my flask from my backpack. I had no appetite for my sandwiches but I was counting on a good shot of caffeine from my strong back coffee providing the kick my senses needed to get me back on an even keel.

I sipped from the flask's detachable cup, watching the area of water immediately in front of me. It was littered with boulders. Dozens and dozens of them, covered in green moss and algae, just visible above the surface. Perhaps in the old days of peat production they had formed the support structure for some sort of wooden platform or jetty?

I imagined stacks of peat piled high there, ready to be loaded onto flat rafts, piloted by men with long poles. I imagined horses and carts waiting on the fringes of the fen for the fuel that would feed the winter fires of the cottages in the surrounding villages. I had no real idea as to the logistics of peat transportation, but imagery was a momentary escape from the anxiety I'd been experiencing.

Then, while focused on the rock that lay closest to the reed bank, I saw something that brought me crashing back down once more. What had appeared to be bevels and crevices on its surface seemed, on closer, inspection to have taken on the features of a human head. Sunken eyes, open mouth, cartilage of the nose almost rotted down to the bone, pronounced nubbins where ears might have been, the entire skull preserved and mummified by the moss and algae.

My heart was pounding. I cast my eyes over the entire archipelago of boulders. A watery Golgotha stretched out before me. Moss furred heads attached to wizened necks and leathery shoulders, chests and upper arms entwined in mermaid stands of duck weed, glittering with gritty slimes of silt.

In a panic I screwed the cup back onto my flask, stuffed it into my backpack and scrambled to my feet. Instantly I experienced that absolute, unfaltering sense that something was again creeping up behind me. I swung around and caught the fleeting glimpse of a shadow streaking behind the black timbers of the wind pump.

I stepped back onto the path. There came the horrible scraping, scuttling sounds of something rapidly scaling the pump. The white sails groaned as they fell through another rotation and, in the gap between them, I saw fully for the first time the hellish creature with designs on me.

Eight muscular but spindly limbs clung grotesquely to the structure of the pump. A torso the size and girth of a large wild boar. Layers of bristly hair that camouflaged it in the colours of the fen, washed out yellow and faded russet infused with streaks of green so dark they were almost black. Multiple glassy eyes punched into her head like studs of onyx. Snaking trails of venom glistening on curving pair of vicious scimitar fangs.

I backed slowly away, fear thumping at my heart, adrenalin sparking in my veins, scarcely able to comprehend what I was seeing. The monstrous spider rose up on her hind quarters and used her four rear limbs to launch herself into the air. She landed a foot or so before me. Her black eyes seemed to bore into my soul. Now she raised her front limbs and brought them crashing down onto the path. Once more a tremor ran through the ground. This time I managed somehow to keep my balance.

I turned and fled.

Almost instantly something wrapped itself around my ankles, hauled me back and sent me crashing to the ground. I heard my nose pop and felt my teeth bite through my lower lip. I coughed and spluttered as blood filled my mouth.

I felt two spidery limbs reach under my hip and shoulder and flip me over. I saw the grotesque creature looming over me, abdomen curved inwards, ejaculating a long silvery strand of spider silk that already securely bound my ankles. I was flipped over again and again, arms flailing like a rag doll. The wind was knocked from my lungs as she relentlessly bound me inside a tight cocoon.

She turned me and turned me and turned me, till finally my arms were clamped to my sides and all that remained clear of the layers of spun silk was my neck and shoulders. In that instant I understood what my fate was to be. Held in this woven trap, immobilized by her venom, sucked dry of my blood and bodily fluids, the husk of my cadaver would be tossed into the cold waters to mummify amongst her innumerate previous victims.

Now that I was fully encased, she flipped me over to gaze upon her quarry, triumphant in her victory. I felt her clammy breath on my face and gagged at the abattoir reek of it. And in those demonic glassy eyes I saw a panoramic tapestry play out. Each eye depicted a different scene. In my head a whispering female voice telepathically relayed an accompanying narrative.

A poor widow with naught to her name but a listing hovel out on the blustery fens. She eked out a living selling herbal concoctions and natural remedies. But a dispute with a neighbour over an alleged stolen ball of yarn had led to her being denounced as a witch.

Men from the village came, fired up by cheap ale and boasts of bravado. They dragged her from her pitiful home, rough hands pushing her head down into the murky fen waters and holding it there till she confessed that *yes - she had occasionally dabbled in the dark arts*.

She was lashed to a pole amidst a pyre of peat set to smoulder so her combustion should be as slow and painful as possible. She spat curses at them. It was then, in midst of the agony that crackled the flesh of her feet like pig skin, she delved deep into her dark knowledge and found the wherewithal to transform herself into the monster which would wreak endless vengeance on the unwary who ventured alone into her territory.

I felt the pain of the flames licking around her ankles. I experienced the agony of her metamorphosis as her body twisted and contorted to its occult induced form. I felt the limbs burrow out from her like bloated worms. I experienced her elation as she fell upon her tormentors and tore them limb from limb.

Now her slavering jaw spread wide. Her head arched back as she prepared to bear down on me and clamp me in her poisonous fangs. I was bound so tight that there was not a single thing I could do to save myself. I tensed and awaited my dreadful fate.

And then.

A miracle.

From somewhere above the fens the steady drone of an engine. I looked skyward in time to see the pale hull of a light aircraft emerging from the clouds, wings outstretched like some white, gliding bird. The widow let out a screech and leapt for the reed bank. I watched the aircraft pass overhead. If the pilot saw me all he'd have been able to discern would be a pile of silver hued weeds bundled on the path.

All too soon it was gone, swallowed by the clouds once more, the engine drone humming away into the distance. And I was alone in the silence that ensued, waiting in abject terror for the widow to return and finish what she'd started, unable to free myself from the layers of silk that bound me as if I was trapped within the bone crushing constrictions of a boa.

By rocking back and forth I managed to roll onto my side. Through the stems of the reeds I could see the mossy heads and torsos slowly sinking back beneath the surface. This had been a demonstration of the widow's power. A deliberate, supernatural surfacing of her victims with the clear intent of unsettling me and instilling fear.

How long now before she came scuttling back to penetrate me with her fangs and immobilise me completely with her venom? Would I be feasted on immediately, or dragged to her lair and snacked upon over an extended period? How long before the hollowed out remnant of me lay deep in the mud, gathering silt and algae?

For a moment the sun came out. A gull landed on me and sat there for a minute or two, as if I was an inanimate object. The sun went behind a cloud again. A shower of squally rain began to drench me. I waited and waited, full of dread and despair, afraid to call out for help in case this was the thing that drew the widow back to me.

I waited.

But she didn't come.

She had no need to rush. I was immobilised. She could come at her leisure.

The notion seized me that I should not give in so easily. I should treat her absence as an opportunity. I recalled how, before I unscrewed the lid from my flask of coffee, I had dropped the little penknife into my pocket, the ones I'd used to wedge out stones from my boots.

I managed to get my thumb far enough into the pocket that I could pull down with sufficient force to rip the seam. A wave of relief washed over me when I discovered the blade had not been pushed completely back down into its housing. It took considerable effort to open the blade. Each time I attempted to squeeze the tip in between my index finger and thumb they slid off. But persistence and perseverance paid off in the end and, with a satisfying click, the blade snapped to full length.

I began to saw at the silk, slowly at first, because I had a minute amount of mobility in my wrist and negligible traction with the blade. I convinced myself that dusk was when the widow would return. That gave me both the reassurance that I had time and also the motivation to work at the silk with relentless urgency.

The afternoon wore on. The rain stopped. The sun fell noticeably lower in the sky. Each time I paused to catch my breath I would peer through reed stems, till finally I saw that all the heads and torso were again fully submerged.

I managed to free my arm and shoulder. From there I managed, heaving and straining to free my other arm, pushing the layers of silk away from me, shuddering at the sticky residue they left behind. The lower half of me was still encased. I set about the remainder of the cocoon with a determined vigour, one hand sawing with the blade, the other ripping at the silk as soon as the gap was wide enough to slide my fingers in.

At last I freed myself entirely. I lay exhausted for a moment amongst the scattered remnants of the cocoon. The wind pump towered over me like some dark sentinel, sails slicing down like executioner's swords. I needed to be away from it, far from the secrets it held for its monstrous mistress.

I rose unsteadily to my feet, bruised and battered from the rough manner in which the widow had rolled me and wrapped me in the imprisonment of her web. The blood from my injured nose was caking over my upper lip. My lower lip was swollen and throbbing from the deep lesion caused by my teeth.

I couldn't face going back in the direction I had come, so I carried on along the route of the circular walk, knowing that it would take me back to Ilkendale. There was a sharp pain in my side, suggesting several ribs may have been cracked by the binding of the silk. My legs felt awkward and disjointed.

The straps of my backpack dug into my shoulders. It felt like a lead weight on my back, a drag anchor, slowing my progress. I removed it, retrieved my binoculars, hung them around my neck, discarded the backpack and moved on. I walked as fast as I could, not wanting to break into jog, determined to reserve whatever energy I could in case I had to run for my life.

The sun was low in the sky. The clouds gathered again. The threat of another downpour seemed imminent. Every time I heard a splash or saw a ripple in the surrounding water, I expected the widow to emerge from the reeds and us her gargantuan form to block my way. At one point three or four ducks rose noisily skyward and flew over my head. My pulse crashed in my ears. My knees almost buckled under me. I thought she had come for me.

I pushed on, determinately focused on the path, pausing every now and then to glance nervously back over my shoulders, scanning the horizon for any sign of the widow's return. I didn't dare to hope that I was actually going to escape. I didn't dare to pause longer than a second or two before I pushed on.

Eventually the rooftops and chimneys of the village cottages came into view. I allowed myself a moment of relief, then I turned and lifted the binoculars to my eyes. I located the wind pump, now tiny in the distance, and turned the little wheel to zoom in and focus. The white sails rose and fell and rose and fell, the black timbers of the construct starkly contrasting the vast expanse of pink that was now blushing the sky.

Then I saw her. She came creeping around the foot of the pump like a she-wolf on the prowl, legs arched as she scuttled with her hirsute abdomen close to the ground. Hands trembling around the binoculars, I watched as she crept forward and examined the shredded cocoon. She rose up on her four hind legs as if she were sniffing the air. I wondered if she could sense me there, watching her. I wondered if her eyes could make out my form. I wondered how fast she could bound on her multiple limbs if she decided to give chase.

I didn't wait to find out.

I turned and fled.

My flight is a naught but blurred memory.

The relief I felt when I fished my car keys from the pocket of my jeans, clambered in and locked all the doors behind me was palpable. I sat there for a long, long time, trembling uncontrollably and weeping into my bruised and scratched hands. I didn't raise the alarm. I didn't knock on someone's door and ask to use their phone. Who could I call? What could I tell them without sounding like someone who had completely lost their senses?

I considered it distinctly possible that some of the residents of Ilkendale would be aware of the existence of the widow. How could you remain unaware if you lived in such close proximity? But they obviously kept their silence. And so, I decided, would I. If, through my inaction, I have condemned others to the terrible fate which almost befell me, then I am culpable and a coward to boot.

Eventually, I summoned the wherewithal to drive home. And here I have stayed, curtains closed and doors locked. There is a new variant on the rise and fresh restrictions in place. I am, therefore, still not required to go in to the office. I order home deliveries of food and necessities. I have no need or desire to venture out of my house.

I sleep badly. Arachnid eyes fill my nightmares. I see, reflected within them, widows burned as witches. I see hideous transformations. I see a night of bloody revenge. I see the centuries topple like dominoes beneath a hunger never sated and a thirst never quenched.

And when I wake in the darkness I hear the eerie timbre of her voice calling in siren song to me over the midnight miles. Her mark is upon me. She is not done with me. Not by far. She beseeches me to return to take my place in that watery grave where her harem of desiccated husbands endlessly nestled in mud and mire sleep their dark, mummified slumber.

And I know that slowly, surely, she is wearing me down, breaking my resistance, bending my will. She will have me in the end. If I am missing now and you are reading this, you will know that I am gone to Ilken Fen.

Arachnid Coalescence

Travis Mushanski

1.

Daniel carefully pulled the pill container out of the shipping box and held it up to the desk light. Across the side of the plastic container was a printed label identifying the sling inside as a *C. Cyaneopubesens.*

"Oh, right on," he muttered to himself, ignoring his daughter impatiently waiting on the other side of the shipping box. "My Green Bottle Blue!"

"Dad," Emma whined. "What is it? Show me."

"Patience, honey." He flashed her a smile. "Hand me that deli container we set up for this little guy. It's time we let him get settled in."

Emma passed the tiny terrarium to Daniel who slowly peeled the top off the pill container to reveal a thick layer of tissue paper. A pair of tweezers helped him carefully pull back the top layer of tissue to reveal the first of eight fuzzy orange legs. Like Emma, the tarantula froze in place. Daniel smiled as he slowly slid the entire roll of tissue into the tarantula's new home. A fine-tipped paintbrush in one hand and the tweezers in the other, Daniel peeled back the tissue to reveal the three-quarter inch baby tarantula.

"Now, Emma," Daniel began in a calm voice, "tarantulas are extremely fragile, especially when they are super tiny like this little guy." The paintbrush carefully touched its tip to each of the sling's toes. With each gentle touch, the arachnid took a cautious step onto the moist coconut fibre substrate. "If you move too fast, or speak too loud, you will spook the sling. It will bolt faster than your eyes could see and before you know it, the tarantula will be lost somewhere in the house." Daniel freed the tissue from the tarantula's enclosure and very pressed the lid into place.

"We should do this on a table," Emma decided. "Can a tarantula jump off a table, Dad?"

Daniel chuckled to himself and ran a hand through her hair. "Oh yeah, they can jump." He lurched at Emma, pretending to be a jumping spider, but his silly attempt was brushed aside by a roll of her eyes. "And that's why we're doing this sitting on the floor. A fall from a table doesn't seem very high, but a tarantula's carapace couldn't handle that much of an impact. It would shatter like glass."

Daniel pulled himself to his feet and put the tarantula's container on his bookshelf next to the other three. A sense of pride washed through him as he read the labels. *Brachypelma albiceps. Caribena versicolor. Tliltocatl albopilosum.*

His concentration was broken when Emma called out, "Oh Dad, there's another one in here!" He spun and cocked his head as he watched her pull a fifth newspaper wrapped container from the shipping box. "And it's a big one," Emma declared as her eyes went wide from amazement.

"Wow, you aren't kidding," Daniel said as he dropped to his knees. "That one's shipping container is larger than the enclosures we built for the others."

He took the container from Emma, surprised at the weight of the object. It was only the size of a small deli container, but must have weighed as much as a brick. "Well, Mom might get mad, but you better run off to the kitchen and grab one of her Tupperware containers. Biggest you can find. We can make him a temporary home for the night." Daniel pointed Emma towards the kitchen with a jerk of his head. "We'll have to make a trip to the pet store to pick up something to house this guy in," he muttered as she ran out of the room.

Daniel twisted the container in his hands to see if there were any distinguishing marks on the packaging material. Just before he gave up, he noticed a small handwritten note on the bottom of the package that read, "FREEBEE". His heart jumped with excitement. *A freebee this big*, he thought, but shrugged his shoulders and began to unwrap the package. Beneath the newspaper was a clear deli container stuffed with paper towel and, despite his best efforts, Daniel couldn't see any sign of what might be inside. Handwritten on the lid of the container was a scientific species name, *P. murispfosa*, with the symbol for the male gender crudely drawn beneath it.

"What does the circle with the arrow on it mean, Daddy?" Emma was leaning over Danielle's shoulder, a large container under her arm.

"It means that whatever is in the package is a male," he explained while sliding a phone out of his pocket. "Can you set that container on the ground, honey? I'm just going to look up this tarantula's species name to see what we're dealing with."

"Can I name him?

"Sure, Emma. No problem." The light from the cell phone illuminated his face, causing distorted shadows to creep into his receding hairline. He scrunched his eyebrows together causing worry lines to crack across his forehead. "Hmm. No results." The phone produced fake clicks as Daniel's fingers hammered away at the virtual keyboard. "Weird. This can't be right."

"Henry!"

"Pardon me?"

"His name is Henry." A smug look flashed across her face. "I decided!"

Daniel shook his head and smiled at Emma. "Of course it is, dear." He set his phone aside. "I'll have to contact Randy tomorrow to find out what he sent us. For now," he paused in midsentence to half-fill the empty Tupperware with substrate. "Let's introduce Henry to his temporary home." He carefully added a cork hide to the rushed enclosure.

He loosened the lid of the deli container the best he could with one hand whilst dipping the entire container into the new enclosure. With slow, even pressure, he pulled the lid off and was pleased nothing stirred inside the container. Using the tweezers, he pulled off a circular chunk of paper towel that was keeping the tarantula out of sight.

With a bit of luck Henry will go right into the cork hide, he thought.

They watched with bated breath as Henry's rear legs and abdomen were revealed. The tarantula had burrowed upside down during shipping. Its abdomen alone was the size of a tennis ball, sporting a deep crimson red colour and its legs, at least five inches in length, were jet black fading towards chocolate brown by its toes. Daniel's heart raced.

It's huge. It's huge and it's gorgeous.

A brief moment of calm cut through the tension of the room as Daniel swapped the tweezers for the paintbrush. With the upmost caution, he gently prodded one of the tarantula's toes and, unlike the other slings, Henry showed no signs of wanting to leave the deli container. With a sigh, Daniel carefully stroked the tarantula's abdomen, but without warning, Henry blindly flicked a cloud of urticating hairs that swam through the air like silvery needles.

Daniel groaned in agony as the fiberglass hairs slammed into his hand, causing him to drop the paintbrush and momentarily lose sight of the tarantula. In a flash, Henry had spun itself around, leapt onto the top of the cork hide and struck out at the deli container with all the force it could muster. Its inch long fangs shredded the edge of the container and Daniel pulled his hand away from the tarantula.

Daniel and Emma knelt, frozen in place, as the tarantula held its ground on the cork hide. Blood trickled down Daniel's wrist from the site of the urticating hairs strike and, despite the intensifying pain, he was able to gesture for Emma to stay as still as possible. The hairs stood up on the back of his neck as the tarantula produced a high pitched hissing noise that reverberated through the room. It reared back into a threat posture, holding its front legs straight up while extending its fangs in Daniel's direction. A hazy fluid dripped from the tip of each fang.

"Whatever you do, honey." Henry bashed his legs onto the cork hide, reminding Daniel to remain silent. "Don't move," he whispered to Emma.

Tears filled her eyes as she remained frozen in place. "But Dad ,I -" Henry spun suddenly and slammed his legs into the edge of the Tupperware container. A long, mournful hiss vibrated out of the tarantula, but the sudden change in its tone broke through the wall of fear that separated Henry and Emma. She wiped the tears from her eyes with her forearm and shakily reached out towards the outstretched legs of the tarantula. Making the peace symbol, she gently placed the tip of her index and ring fingers against the tips of Henry's tarsal claws.

Daniel was about to call out for Emma to run when time seemed to stop. Henry and Emma were locked in an eternal embrace that knew no bounds. Their fingers and toes locked together as Emma's breathing slowed. A sense of harmony erased her fear. At the same time, Henry retracted his fangs and brushed his chelicerae with his pedipalps with a sense of contentment. Once the embrace had ended, Henry slowly climbed up Emma's arm to her shoulder. Once there, he caressed her neck with his abdomen as he carefully performed a circular dance on her shoulder. Emma gazed at the tarantula on her shoulder and smiled.

2

Billy Eilish stood in front of the dilapidated bungalow, staring at the smudged address scribbled across the palm of his hand. The house number matched what his teacher, had written, but he couldn't imagine Emma living in a dump like this. The windows were blocked with yellowed newspaper, the cedar plank siding was spackled with dense clumps of mold and the screen door fluttered in the wind. On either side of the broken front path, dry dandy soil was held in place by a lawn of stinging nettle.

"Well, buddy, should we get this over with?" Billy asked the Boston terrier sitting impatiently at his side. He let out a high pitched bark and returned to panting, his tongue hanging out of his mouth. Billy bent down, rubbed the dog between its ears and slung his backpack over his shoulder.

The late afternoon sun beat down on the two as they traversed the broken pathway to the front door of the house. The terrier was quite content to follow in the cool shade of Billy's shadow, pausing only briefly to peer around his owner at the sound of the screen door smashing into the door casings. They reached the steps to the front patio, where the Boston terrier snorted violently and plunked his ass down with a muted growl.

"Brave to the end, hey, bud?" Billy shook his head and chuckled. "Just be sure to watch my rear. Thanks, champ!" The dog buried his face in his paws and lifted his big brown eyes to watch his master.

Billy knocked three times and had to brush white paint from his knuckles which came off the door like a powdery mildew. The sound of something crashing to the floor inside the house made Billy jump back in time for him to see the porch light come to life. There was a drawn-out electrical crackle that ended up with the lightbulb burning out. The dog gave a series of high-pitched yips before Billy held up a hand to calm him down.

"It's ok, Tucker," he said as calmly as his heart would allow him. "Calm down, bud."

He was about to knock a second time when he heard a raspy voice call out from inside the house. "Come in. It's open."

A ghastly silence filled the world around Billy and a shiver ran up his spine. He shook off the bad feeling and pushed the door open. The moment the door opened there was a violent rush of hot air as if the house was hermetically sealed. When the air pressure equalized, the stale musty aroma wafted out the front door. Billy sensed it dive into his lungs, causing an itchy sensation to cling to the walls of his esophagus. He coughed to find relief, but there was none to be found.

"Hello," he called into the house. He cautiously pushed the door into the dimly lit foyer. His eyes had trouble focusing in the poor light of the house. "Mrs. Hill sent me to bring Emma some homework to catch up on."

"Ah. Yes," the raspy voice drifted around the corner, seemingly beckoning Billy to follow. "We called on her behalf." There was a shuffle of chairs

71

and an incandescent light flickered to life around the corner from Billy.

The shadows pushed past Billy as he pursued the source of the voice. He rounded the corner and his jaw dropped at the ghoulish tableau before him. The source of the voice, an impossibly thin, middle-aged man with disheveled white hair, sat staring straight ahead into a newspaper covered window. His arms dangled at his sides as if atrophy had long ago set in. His head was tilted at an unnatural angle and his body quivered with each surprised gulp of air.

"Thanks for coming, boy." It came from somewhere within the hollow man. His lips barely trembled as the words slipped out of his mouth. "We've been waiting." His voice trailed off into a wheeze.

Billy's muscles tensed when he noticed the woman sprawled out across the kitchen table. Her arms were wrapped in a circle around her head. She was face down on the table. Large sores seeped clear yellowish fluid where large clumps of white hair had been torn off the scalp. Billy watched her back sporadically rise and fall off the surface of the table, but otherwise, she showed no signs of consciousness.

"Honey, your little friend is here," a melodic voice rang out from the darkest depths of a cavern. It bounced off the walls and reverberated through the house.

Billy watched in horror as the stifling silence began to suck the life out of the house. The walls pulsed as they bent and warped inward, drawing the contents of the building together. The heat rose to the point of suffocation, causing Billy to turn into a boy sized clump of melting clay. The backpack hanging off his shoulder pulled with all its might to slowly slice the boy in half. The hollow figures turned their dead eyes to Billy. Yellow light shined through their transparent skin. They both wore distorted smiles and somewhere far beyond their husk bodies, a joyous roar of laughter spilled out into the world.

The sound of shoes click-clacking across the hardwood floors restored the home and its inhabitants to their original state. The sudden snap back to normalcy made Bill's knees buckle and he had to catch the edge of the kitchen table to prevent collapsing into the hollow man.

"Oh Billy, you made it!" Emma dashed across the floor and wrapped her arms around him. She wore a bright yellow sundress that twirled behind her and a bright orange headband tied her hair back. She was so giddy with joy she was nearly vibrating.

Billy blushed with embarrassment and after stumbling over his words, he managed, "Well, it looks like you're feelin' better." He awkwardly glanced towards the two figures at the kitchen table and a barely audible "Ahhhh" dribbled out of his mouth.

"Oh, I'm sorry." She pantomimed the words. "Did I not introduce you to my mother and father?"

"You can call me Daniel." The male figure's head made a sharp jerk up and down. Its voice was jovial and kind now, yet it was still a mile away.

73

"And this lovely lady," Emma slumped onto the back of the woman on the table, "is my mom, Sarah." The woman let out an agonized groan as Emma giggled.

Bang! Bang! Bang!

The sound of a shotgun blasts erupted out of the far end of the house. The building shook on its foundations, sending anything not screwed down smashing to the ground. Billy fell onto Daniel and they both tumbled to the floor.

Bang! Bang! Bang!

There was a sudden scramble of claws on hardwood floor as Tucker skidded past the kitchen, trying to get traction. "Tucker, no!" Billy called out to the terrier as he pulled himself out from under the dead weight of Emma's father. He dragged himself across the floor on his hands and knees, but he wasn't fast enough to grab the dog before he bounded down the hallway.

Before Billy could blink, there was a heavy thud and an ear-piercing yelp. The terrier disappeared beneath an object so large that it absorbed all the light from the home. The thing was a vast living shadow. The scratching of the terrier's feet stilled with a gruesome crunch of bones breaking under immense pressure. Through blurry eyes, Billy watched the great black void slide his best friend out of view.

He dashed down the hallway and tried to force his way into a room at the end of the hall. The door snagged on something on the floor and refused to budge. A thick layer of silk laced across the threshold of the room like a carpet. Billy dropped

74

his shoulder and drove his weight into the door. There was a loud tear as the silk ripped apart, sending him flailing past the doorway.

Billy pulled himself up to a kneeling position and froze as he scanned the room. The yellow light filtering through the newspaper slathered window showcased a room full of silk spider webs. They formed circular patterns across the walls and ceiling. As he shifted his weight from knee to knee, he realized the pillow soft floor was made up of thousands of tiny layers of spider silk. Across from Billy was a web tunnel that spiraled into the rear of the room and in the other corner was a bulbous clump of webs that pulsed rhythmically in the shadows.

"Tuk? Tuk? Is that you, buddy?" Billy whispered into the shadows of the room. He inched his way across the room on his hands and knees, his palm crunched into a chrysalis tethered to the floor.

He fought the urge to vomit and slowly pulled his hand out of the object as quietly as he could. Long trails of clear mucus ran through his fingers that desperately clung to his skin. Billy held his hand up to the window and could see hair of varying lengths and tiny chips of white stone mixed into the substance. He let out a panicked squeal as he gazed into the brown cocoon: It was full of discarded bones, teeth and hair.

"It's called a bulus." A calm, monotone voice cut through Billy's growing terror.

He spun around to see Emma standing in the doorway holding a large butcher knife. He scrambled across the floor towards her and reached out to grab hold of her leg. "It got him, Emma," Billy muttered while he glanced over his shoulder into the blackness of the web tunnel. "We have to save him! We have to -"

Emma brushed his hand off her leg and casually walked past. "You see," Emma continued, oblivious to Billy's distress, "when a tarantula eats, it injects digestive enzymes into their prey to liquefy its body." She used the butcher knife to sort through the bulus that Billy had smashed. "In the end, it just drinks its prey like a big milkshake." A smile smeared its way across her face. She looked back to Billy and added, "All that's left is a pile of bones."

"Emma, what the hell are you talking about?" Billy was standing now, holding his head in his hands. His wide eyes were filling with tears and a tremble rippled through his jawline.

"Shhh. Can you hear them?" Emma traced the ceiling with her gaze until she found her way to the pulsing mass in the corner of the room. "Hundreds of tiny voices calling out my name in the darkness," Emma explained in a hushed monotone.

Billy watched in silent horror as Emma meandered towards the great webbed mass and casually stretched her body out across it. Bulbous lumps formed in its surface and began to ripple around Emma's body. The entire mass lifted her up and down as if taking in great breaths.

"My Dad was wrong." Bliss washed over Emma. "Henry is actually a female." She lifted the knife above her head and plunged it into the mass beneath her. The thing went still as she dragged the blade across its surface. She traced the deep gash with her neatly trimmed fingernails. Then Emma carefully dug her fingers into the sliced webbing and peeled the layers apart. With each gentle tug, tiny sets of silver legs reached out of the egg sack. In moments, dozens of tarantula nymphs emerged, sporting silver legs and semi-transparent, olive-green abdomens.

Billy took a step forward to pull Emma away from the hatching tarantulas, but before he could take a second step, his chest erupted in a pink mist of blood. Dozens of two-foot-long urticating hairs struck their target while dozens more passed straight through. He exhaled and fell to his knees. Blood trickled from his mouth as he stared into Henry's eight beady black eyes.

A cool hand brushed Billy's auburn hair out of his eyes as he coughed a spray of congealing blood onto his midsection. Without lifting his head, he rolled his eyes up to stare into Emma's grinning face.

"The children are hungry." Beyond the deep black gouges of exhaustion under her eyes, tears filled her vision as joy emanated from every pore of her body. "You will be one with us now," she decreed. She gently kissed him on the forehead.

Emma stepped back to stand on guard with her hand on Henry's carapace. They watched in silence as the spiderlings, little more than eggs with legs, smothered Billy's body without interference. The first hundred bites fired crippling pain through his nervous system. Once the venom worked its way into his bloodstream, it wasn't long before all of his capillaries, veins, and internal organs melted into a primordial stew.

3

The residential suburb slumbered beneath the pale light of the crescent moon. Dreams drifted in and out of windows on the wings of the cool fall breeze. It gently caressed the cheeks of children and adults alike. Just as they would any other evening, a myriad of insects and rodents bustled through their insignificant existence, creating a foundation chorus that humanity builds its life upon.

Like all things in the ever-expanding universe, change is the only aspect of life that is a constant. In time, all cultures inevitably end, continents collapse into the ocean and stars will eventually supernova. The precise moment of these events is often triggered by the slightest variation of everyday life. In the case of humanity, a cosmic change occurred when the front door of a dilapidated bungalow eased itself open.

Silence abruptly filled neighborhood as the creatures of the night took notice of the shifting paradigm. As swift as the silence came, the evacuation of life drew a distressed pulse as it fled away from ground zero. In only moments, the foundation chorus of humanity was destroyed.

An enormous black tarantula stepped out onto the front porch from the darkness of the house. Emma stood next to the Great Dane sized creature stroking its flame-coloured abdomen. The yellow sundress was soiled and tattered, yet it shimmered as it fluttered in the evening breeze. The thrum of its heartbeat vibrated through Emma as it matched pace with her own.

The pair walked down the crumbling pathway and a low steady chittering emanated from deep within the dilapidated house. The sound reached its crescendo and a flood of tarantulas spilled out from the open door into the night. Their pitch-black bodies reflected the silvery moonlight as they dashed away from their home, led only by their hunger and need to survive. In the darkness of the evening, they will feed upon family pets, then quickly graduate to feasting on small children, and eventually consume all human life. Nothing can sustain their insatiable hunger.

With The Coming Of The Night

Dorothy Davies

Early sun shines through heavy mist, each droplet pure white, hanging low, bejewelling plants and trees alike, decorating webs, spangling grass. A summer day.

There is a closeness; a feeling, a promise of heat to come touching us, our senses quiver in anticipation and expectation.

It is time.

Us hunters must leave our quarters, our armour cleaned, we thrust our jaws aggressively forward; stiff collars protect our vulnerable necks. We pass the vigilant guards who look us over once and wave us on. In the dense undergrowth we split up, searching for places to hide, to await our prey. A platoon has gone to seek the many legged ones, they who give sweetness at a touch, checking that they are safe from enemies.

The many legged ones are our very own, we will brook no interference.

Always there is the desperate overwhelming need for food, food for us who hunt and for those who remain behind. There is an important role for everyone in the colony, from those guarding the entrances to those who nurse the *Almost Born* and tend the *Legless* and the *Enclosed.* There are those who do nothing more than flaunt their wings and look for the coming of the *Day* but these too must be fed, for their role in our survival is essential. We who hunt have a heavy job to do to feed them all and we know it.

Safe in a concealed place, we can rest for a moment and wait. Behind us, in the colony, the attendants will be cleaning and turning the *Almost Born* so they will know they are safe. The *Legless* will be asking for food and if it is to be hot, for their attendants to hook their hairs together and carry them to a higher chamber, so they might luxuriate in the warmth of the day, and grow.

Today is the *Day*.

No one has indicated in any way it is the *Day* and yet we know. It is perhaps that sense of urgency that has swept through the colony, or a feeling in the stifling heat of the day that tells us. Whatever it is, we know.

Today, the *Winged Ones* will fly.

Even as we continue our patient wait for food, or forage in the dangerous open spaces, they will flare their wings in the sultry heat and fly for the first – and last – time. In flying they will meet and in a locking together of bodies there will be the giving and receiving of life, future generations, continuation of the race, survival of the colony. This was the *Day* of the consummation of the future. Jealous? No, we have our own role to play. It is for others to see to the future while we attend to the present.

Battle is joined! The word is out! With armour in place, we go forth into the light, kill or be killed, there is no quarter given or asked. Razor sharpness severs limbs, decapitates enemies and ourselves alike and the defeated flee from our onslaught. We take home the bodies of the dead and dying, there will be food for all this special *Day*.

Hot rains came.

They came so suddenly from a sky clear and bright, destroying our earthworks, sending scalding mud and burning water through the myriad tunnels. We rush madly in sheer panic, we try to reinforce vulnerable defences, Many are suffocated under steaming collapsing walls. The Winged Ones have hidden themselves in deep chambers and hope the burning flood will pass them by. On them depends our future.

When the rains stop we find many have perished. The joy in the *Day* has gone and in its place comes sorrow and despair, There are demolished walls and chambers and many, many bodies. We scramble over the remains, searching for the living, ignoring the dead. As the other hunters return we tell them to stay and help. We need all the help we can get. There is food enough for now; we can eat the dead.

Our first job is to clear the halls, so the Winged Ones can walk. No matter what we feel, this is the day for which the whole colony has worked and waited, nothing can stand in the way of the *Flight*.

The sun rises high, pouring down life-giving heat, scorching the earth, drying up the surface devastation of the hot rains. But deep within there is much to grieve over: the loss of *Almost Born*, of *Legless* lost in the higher chambers where they had been taken. Some of the *Enclosed* are gone, buried in their own chambers. And in some of the deep chambers, *Winged Ones* lay still, caught by the flood, lost on the very threshold of their *Day*.

With the coming of the evening there are huge thunder clouds, piling high into the darkening blueness, obscuring the light, oppressing the atmosphere, dulling the senses of all but those of us for whom time is standing still.

The *Winged Ones* are ready, claws clicking, bodies shining, wings smooth, their multi-faceted eyes flashing in the semi darkness.

The time grows close. The tension builds. Then, as if by a signal, for no one has made a sound, the *Winged Ones* begin to move toward the now unguarded entrances, seared shapeless by the hot rains. Their wings quiver in the subdued light. They move, pressing together, long lingering moments of awareness before the *Flight*. Then, even as we look, they soar into the air, claws close to their bodies, wings spreading to catch the thermals that send them spinning giddily into flight. In a huge cloud of wings they find one with which to mate, locking together, giving, receiving, all knowledge, all life, one moment of ecstasy and insanity.

Even as we below watch, many die. Even in *Flight* they are taken by greater predators, bolder hunters than we, snatched from the air. Some fly into poisonous clouds. In passion they are blind.

We wait.

We watch them fall, locked together, crashing back to earth, lying on the warm ground in love, As her partner dies, she moves away, ripping at her wings, tearing them from her body, casting them aside. To us, they are gossamer teardrops, cried for those who had given – and died.

With the coming of the night, when the last ones have gone deep into the ever comforting embrace of the earth, we return to our sad, lonely, depleted colony. There is much to do, rebuilding, repairing, giving birth all over again.

There is always tomorrow for us busy garden ants.

Out Of Hiding

Paul Edwards

Aaron crouched beside the spider's web, scowling, grimacing at it. He flicked the spark wheel of his lighter, holding the flame close to the web. The strands swiftly began to shrivel and shrink, blackening toward the creature at their centre.

The patio door slid open. "What *are* you doing?" Leanne asked, fractiously.

The spider dropped to the ground, righted itself and scurried off beneath the fence.

Aaron straightened, sliding his lighter into the front pocket of his jacket. She glared and glared as though she expected him to do something, say something. Instead, feeling stupid and small, he averted his gaze toward the overgrown grass in their garden.

More webs glinted in the sunlight.

***

Aaron stumbled into the house, wet through from rain. He took off his shoes and folded his coat over the radiator to dry.

He heard faint, giggly voices coming from the front room. Leanne had invited her friend, Sharon, around for the afternoon, he remembered, suddenly. He drifted into the kitchen, grabbed an open bottle of Merlot and poured himself a large glass. He didn't want to go into the front room; didn't like Sharon, or the way Leanne changed whenever she was around her.

The door to the front room stood ajar. Aaron went toward it, glass in hand, listening.

"How did you feel when you heard?"

"Weird. It was *so* long ago. Yet in some ways, it feels like yesterday."

Aaron shrank back toward the fridge. He opened its door and helped himself to a piece of leftover chicken. Made a point of slamming the door shut.

"Aaron?" Leanne called. "You home?"

"Yes," he said then mumbled under his breath, "who else were you expecting?"

He turned from the fridge just as a spider came scuttling out from under the table, disappearing into the gap beneath the cooker. It was large and fat, with a distinctive white streak on its back.

Aaron gulped his wine, rinsed the glass out, then reluctantly made for the front room.

Leanne and Sharon stopped giggling as soon as he entered.

"Hi, Sharon." He waved stiffly at her.

"Hi, Aaron."

"How was work?" Leanne asked.

"Same old, same old."

He stood in silence, trying to think of something else to say. Leanne looked bemused, almost embarrassed for him. "I'm going to go dry off," he said at last.

Leanne nodded, "Sure." Then, as he was leaving, added: "We were talking about organising a party. I was thinking we could have it here."

"Sounds great," he lied, passing through the door, closing it behind him and heading sullenly for the stairs.

***

Later that evening, as they lay in bed together, Leanne turned to him and asked, "You okay?"

He lowered his Kindle, glancing warily up at her. "Why wouldn't I be?"

"You seem quiet. Tense, even."

Something twitched and scratched restlessly at the back of his skull. He set his Kindle down on the duvet. "I'm knackered," he said. "I'll feel better if I get my eight hours in, I'm sure."

She turned her attention back to her phone, tapping the screen with her finger.

"Who you messaging?" he asked.

She turned her phone toward herself so he couldn't see. "No one. Friends. About the party we're going to have next Friday."

He hitched the covers up around his shoulders, then shifted his body away from her. She muttered something, but he didn't hear, wasn't bothered by what she had to say.

Something caught his attention beyond the open bedroom door, something as big as a fist, crouched down in a wedge of light cast by a streetlamp outside.

It had a white streak on its back. Long, prickly legs. Twitching and bristling, growing steadily before his eyes.

Aaron buried his head beneath his pillow. Should he say something? No—he felt too awkward, too embarrassed to broach it with Leanne.

When he looked again, the thing had gone. He knew it wouldn't have gotten very far.

He needed to confront it, he realised. Kill it. Before it could get any bigger.

***

Aaron and Leanne took their usual morning stroll into town on Saturday, squeezing and bustling their way through the crowds.

They entered a café, chose a table beneath a print of Van Gogh's *Sunflowers*. They took off their coats, folded them over the backs of the chairs. Sat down and waited in silence to be served.

Aaron remembered a time when they used to enjoy chatting. These days they seemed to have so very little to talk about.

They drank their lattes and ate brioches smeared with butter and jam. People jostled and squirmed past the windows. She mentioned the party again, which irked. Said quite a few of their friends were coming. Aaron had few friends of his own. The ones he did have he shared with Leanne, who liked her better than him, he felt.

She set her coffee mug down on the table. "You didn't need to come out, Aaron. If you're feeling unwell, you should've stayed home."

"I'm okay," he sniffed. "It's just so busy out. Overwhelming, you know?"

"Why don't you go for a run when we get back? You always feel better after a run."

They gathered up their coats and paid the bill a short while later. They were pulling open the door when a man stepped up to come through. He had slicked-back hair with a white streak running through it. He looked surprised when he saw Leanne. "Leanne?" he said. "My God!" He laughed brightly, beaming from ear-to-ear. "Wow, it's been so long."

She laughed, too, clearly flustered because her cheeks and throat had flushed red. "Simon," she said. "You're back."

He stepped outside as they did, lingering under the café's wide canopy. He pushed his hands into his pockets, rocking backwards and forwards on his heels. "It's funny how things work out. Or don't, in my case."

"It's great to see you again," Leanne smiled.

"You too."

"Were you just going in?"

"Was going to grab a coffee. This place any good?"

"Best café in town." She glanced round at Aaron. "Oh, this is Aaron. Aaron, meet Simon." Simon smiled awkwardly and held out his hand. Aaron shook it, briefly. "We go way back, Simon and I."

Aaron smiled, but couldn't bring himself to say anything.

"I got your invitation," Simon said.

Leanne beamed. "Great. You coming?"

"Yeah. It'll be cool to see everyone again."

"Fantastic." She giggled self-consciously, twirling her hair around her forefinger. "See you Friday, then."

He nodded. "Looking forward to it."

Simon raised his hand and gave a departing wave, then pushed through the door into the café. The colour slowly shrank from Leanne's face.

"Who's he?" Aaron asked as they dodged down a side street to avoid the crowds.

"An old friend." She zipped her jacket up to her throat. "There was a group of us. We used to hang out all the time." She chewed her lip as if deliberating over what to say next. "You'll like him," she said, eventually.

They didn't speak again until they arrived home. It was Leanne's turn to withdraw; he couldn't even begin to imagine what she was thinking about. Or perhaps he could—ideas formed inside his mind that he didn't like so much.

Soon she started talking about the party again—what they needed to buy; how the house could be rearranged; where they could put people up if they decided to sleep over. Aaron had had enough. He told her he was going for that run, got changed and left.

***

Two nights before the party he experienced a strange and unsettling dream. He was on his way to the party, walking along an empty street toward his house. He felt inexplicably anxious, worrying over how he might impress Leanne that night.

He reached the front door, rapped loudly with his knuckles. Leanne opened it, blinking, smiling at him. "Aaron," she said. "How lovely to see you." She was wearing the dress he liked her in, the black one with the V neck and tassels. She beckoned him in. He heard music playing from the front room. It was a song he knew Leanne loved, but he hated—a generic pop number whose title eluded him. Guests were talking and laughing in the front room, but whenever he tried to look at them, he saw only their shadows, fluttering and flickering across the walls.

"Have you met Simon?" Leanne asked and then Simon appeared behind her, his arms wrapped around her waist. The white streak in his hair appeared more prominent and he grinned at Aaron as she said: "We go way back, Simon and I."

Aaron noticed Simon's face was convulsing, like there was something under the skin trying to break out...

Aaron gasped awake, rising, coughing and spluttering. Leanne sat up, too. She put the flat of her hand on his spine, rubbing it in soft, circular motions. "You okay? Whatever's the matter?"

His jaw was aching, pain tearing up both sides of his face to his ears. He rubbed his jaw, wondering if he'd been grinding his teeth again.

He cast back the duvet, tramped downstairs. Filled the kettle and snatched a mug from out of the cupboard over the sink. The sun was beginning its ascent, through the window it was painting the kitchen walls with its fiery hue.

91

Leanne joined him at their dining table a short while later, wrapped in her dressing gown and with her hair hanging in dishevelled ribbons in front of her face.

"Do you want some coffee?" he asked.

She shook her head.

He touched his jaw again. "My face aches like fuck. My jaw hurts, all around here. I feel sick, too."

"I'm worried about you," she said. "Sounds like a symptom of stress to me. I really think you should make a doctor's appointment."

He ran a finger around the rim of his coffee mug.

"I rang your Mum the other day," she said and he looked up in surprise. "She told me about your... phobias, shall we say? How they developed into delusions, Aaron. Things got bad when your parents split, right?" He didn't know what to say to that; he just kept quiet, staring at his hands clasped together in his lap.

She flashed him a sad, tired smile. "I know you had help before. Perhaps it's worth you seeking some again?"

Suddenly, she seemed exasperated by his silence.

"It's you," she snapped. "The poison in your body and mind, polluting the landscape! It's not the outside world at all; you're perfectly safe, you know. You're your own worst enemy, you always were."

He wasn't even sure if he was hearing her properly—it could quite easily be his mother speaking, not Leanne at all.

92

Leanne rose and swept out of the kitchen, slamming the door behind her. Her words had washed over him. He hadn't seen the thing in days.

But he knew what it was.

Knew where it was hiding, too.

***

"Help me move this, Aaron." It was the afternoon of the party. Aaron joined Leanne in the utilities room and together they cleared a stack of items from off the floor: a sack of charcoal; a rusted bicycle; a bottle of lighter fluid; a crate of old books. Aaron squeezed and sidled past her, then lifted and carried a table out to the front room.

"Do you think we'll need the other one?" Leanne asked, glancing at the second fold-out table standing up against the wall in the corner.

"If we need it," Aaron called, "I'll grab it later, okay?"

They were soon locked in their own separate worlds, Leanne rearranging the furniture, Aaron cooking and preparing the food out in the kitchen. He wasn't afraid, he realised; he knew its plans and intentions. He mustn't keep letting these things scuttle away from him because they only came back bigger and uglier in the end.

When people began arriving, Aaron kept busy prepping the food, pouring drinks, washing up after himself, which pissed Leanne off immensely. At one point he glanced down at the space between floor and cooker and remembered when it had been small enough to hide in there. Not now, though.

He carried serving platters and bowls of nibbles on a tray into the front room. Leanne, Sharon and Simon were standing in a corner, laughing at something Simon had said. Leanne was reaching up to stroke Simon's face; "...always the best," he was sure he heard her say.

Aaron set the food down on the coffee table, turned and pushed his way back into the kitchen. Something in his head was scratching, rustling; interfering with his thoughts and mood. He mustn't stall, he thought. Mustn't lose sight of what he had to do today. She needed to know—there was no way he could allow this to go on; for his sake as well as hers.

He felt oddly displaced when he returned to the front room and had to blink several times in an effort to anchor himself. He marched over to Leanne, gripping her arm and turning her to him. "We do need that other table," he said. She sipped her wine, gazing at him through intoxicated eyes. "Simon," he sighed, turning to him. "Would you mind...?"

Simon glanced at Leanne, shrugged. "No problem."

Aaron led him out of the front room and down the hall, the scratching intensifying inside his skull. They walked past the downstairs bathroom, its door open, their forms passing by in the mirror on the wall. Aaron reached the utilities room, ushered Simon inside. Quietly closed the door behind them both.

The noise in Aaron's head was ferocious now, blocking out all other sounds.

Simon turned to him and paled.

"I know what you are," Aaron said, flatly.

Before Simon could reply, Aaron shoved him hard, sending him flying into the wall, sliding down it with blazing eyes. *"...the fuck?"*

Aaron seized the lighter fluid, unscrewed it. Threw the contents over Simon and then spat on him. Simon fought to get up, but Aaron forced him to the floor with a swift kick and stamp of his foot. Aaron tipped out the remainder of the bottle, then scrambled through his pockets for his lighter.

One flick, two flicks of the wheel, and then there was flame—Simon gasped, fire racing up his arm at speed.

"You *fuck*—" Simon managed, but then his midriff was on fire too and Aaron swung himself around and burst out of the room to evade the flames. Simon charged but Aaron's sleeved hands shoved him again, sending him spiralling into the hall, kicking, writhing and screaming. Then Simon was up onto his feet, scurrying toward the front room, shrieking at the top of his lungs as flames consumed his entire body.

Everyone was screaming now and, as Aaron fell against the wall, he watched their guests dash past, clamouring for the exit. From where he was standing, he could see bright orange serpents writhing all over the curtains in the front room.

Leanne stumbled out into the hall, gasping, sobbing hysterically. He seized her arms, turned her to him. Her eyes were huge and wide, filled with an emotion he had never seen in her before. He could hear a long, agonised wail echoing throughout the house, but didn't bat an eyelid.

"Stay," he shouted. "*I'm* here. There mustn't be anyone… nobody else, Leanne."

She began to squirm and fight, stark terror carved into her features.

He tried to pull her close, but she broke free of him and ran.

"You don't know what it was!" he shrieked after her. "What was hiding!"

She flew out of the door, howling and screaming at the world. He turned and started toward the front room, wanting to see it reveal itself. But his stomach was sick and he found it hard to breathe. Something was blocking the passage of his throat, rising thickly, swiftly toward his twitching, swelling mouth. He resumed walking, spluttering, coughing and retching. Then, pausing, twisting wildly around, he focused his gaze on his face reflected in the bathroom mirror.

His image gagged as it glared back at him. Desperately, he wanted to howl, to scream, but he couldn't because his face was convulsing and there was an enormous spider's leg emerging from his open mouth.

When Worlds Collide

Jason R. Frei

The world came apart at the intersection of New and Church Streets. I was sitting at a red light, head bopping to The Ramones. "Twenty, twenty, twenty-four hours to go-o-o. I wanna be sedated".

The music pulsed through the car and synced perfectly with the beating of my heart, the slapping of the windshield wipers, the blink-blink-blink of the turn signal. That's when the shift occurred. One minute, sitting at a light. The next, a key turned and a door opened on creaking hinges.

That other world was much older, darker. It was full of shadows and fear.

I was sitting in my car on a rainy afternoon and then I wasn't. I was sitting on top of my car and the gloomy daylight turned into a velvet night, or at least a facsimile of it. It was dark, but the stars were different, younger, closer.

I stared down from the roof of the car as quicksilver snakes slithered across the street. They flowed like mercury, each scale undulating with the movement, rising and falling one after the other. They reflected light from every source - the sodium headlights of my car, the pinpricks of newborn stars, the feeble yellow of the overhead streetlamps.

While the snakes flooded the tarmac river of road, a drumming filled my ears like the beating blades of a thousand Black Hawk helicopters. There appeared above me a great multi-hued dragonfly, its whip-thin body polished like stainless steel. It darted up and down the road, picking up snakes in its razor tipped claws and stuffed them, still wriggling, into its terrible red maw.

I dove under the car as the beast's compound honeycomb eyes searched me out and instilled in me a feeling of trypophobia. My stomach lurched and cold sweat ran freely down my face. The snakes hissed in their whispery tongues and glided toward me, twining over and under me to escape the monster from above.

I grabbed them by the handful and threw them from under the car, a sacrifice to the winged creature that sought my demise. Its droning increased in response to my supplication. While it gorged on the silvery snacks, I darted out and ran to the nearest building.

The buildings in this world were odd, jarring in their architecture. They jutted out of the ground like a bare knuckle boxer's teeth, skewed and cracked and broken. They were colored in dull grays, pale yellows and sickly greens. Doors were set irregularly into the walls, some at impossible angles or wrapped around the corners of the buildings. Windows were lifeless and though light showed through them, nothing could be seen inside.

I ran to the nearest door that fit my ideal concept, being that it was upright and in the middle of a wall. It swung open soundlessly and I bounded through into some sort of otherworldly dojo.

The floor was covered in foamy mats emitting no sound as I trod on them. Mirrors lined one wall, but the images they reflected were of no objects in this room. I approached one, but it was not my reflection that looked back. A small girl giggled and waved from the other side. When I did not return the wave, she scowled, her face darkening. She flipped me the middle finger and stormed off.

The studio smelled of sweat, musty incense and fried vegetables. There was a fine layer of dust on everything. No, not dust, maybe pollen? It was a yellowish sticky residue.

I approached a small Italian man with a bushy mustache. The sensei stared at me with unblinking beady black eyes. His arms were crossed, as was his face. There were serrated edges on the undersides of his arms from elbow to wrist. I opened my mouth to speak, but he sliced the air with one impossibly sharp hand. He pointed to the back of the studio, indicated a door, nodded his head and grunted.

His voice was impossibly deep and its tone set my teeth on edge. "Go, outsider, before you are caught."

The door was unassuming, an otherwise normal door in an abnormal world. I opened it and stepped into a janitor's closet filled with mops, buckets and shelves of cleaning supplies. The back wall was a forest of bamboo.

The green stalks towered above the walls where no ceiling could contain them. A steady wind blew, causing a dry rustling and clacking to fill the room. It made me think of wind chimes set with bones instead of metal. Small pinpricks of flashing light winked off and on through the stalks.

I pushed through the forest, bending the tightly knitted trees out of my way and fell unexpectedly into a smoky noodle-scented arcade. It appeared empty save for the flickering colored pixels and the whistles, beeps and clangs from the machines. I heard a whirring behind me, turned and glimpsed the gossamer hem of a dress flow around a corner.

I chased after and saw the ephemeral outlines of the ghosts in the machines as they played long after their fingers could no longer hold the tokens, grip the joysticks or stab the buttons. I ran headlong out of the arcade through a set of grimy glass doors.

I emerged into the daybreak of this world. The glare of a red sun, like the baleful eye of a dreadful god, filtered down through clouds of dust and tendril wisps of smoke. It burned my eyes like acid and left a bitter trail down the back of my throat. Small fires dotted the landscape. Noises assaulted me from every direction- chittering and clacking, droning and buzzing, hissing and spitting.

A column of ants, twice the size of me, marched past in their glossy black armor. A chorus of crickets erupted from a nearby corner, their bowed arms sawing a discordant and unsettling melody. Overhead, a squadron of hornets screamed past, their blurred wings causing my eyes to water. I hid amongst the shadows and slowly crept down the dangerous street.

These sights were alarming, but nothing prepared me for the scene laid out in the square ahead. Humans crowded together in cages, their clothes shredded and filthy. Blood flowed across the ground, making it slick and crimson-tinged. They looked dejected, defeated, hopeless.

One of them spotted me and pointed. Soon, the entire throng was shouting and banging on the bars of their cages, beckoning for me to come and rescue them. Above their din grew a fearful hissing. Strands of webbing dropped from the tops of the cages, encasing the hysterical horde. A large spindly-legged spider climbed down in front of them. Its bloated body was black with splotches of terrible yellows and reds. It turned toward me and I could see my fear reflected in the mirrors of its myriad eyes.

Above the din, I heard one of the less capacitated humans yell for me to run. I dashed down a narrow alley and became lost in the maze of the terrible city. Overhead, I could hear the skittering of my pursuers.

I turned a corner and slid to a halt as a wall loomed in front of me. I turned to retrace my steps, but was too late. A silky rope shot to the ground in front of me and stuck fast. I looked up as a fat mottled gray spider swiftly made its descent. It had bristles over its body and its mandibles clacked and drooled as it approached, hatred and death gleaming in its eyes.

I backed up against the wall and pressed myself into it, hoping for some reprieve. The spider advanced and towered over me. It whispered promises of agony and slow pain. I raised my arm over my face and felt myself fall backwards.

I started as a glaring horn sounded from behind me. My eyes snapped open and the traffic light before me glowed green. Phosphorescent lights flashed twice behind me in rapid succession. I eased my car around the corner, put on my blinkers and pulled over.

My hands shook and my mouth was bone dry. I thrust open the car door and vomited bright splashes of stomach acid onto the pavement. I got out of the car and looked around at this world, my world. I breathed in the air and felt the cooling splash of rain on my face. Images of that other world burned and blurred in my brain, but I was home and safe.

I turned to get back in the car when a shadow scuttled across its roof and then stopped. Eight eyes stared back at me from a gray bristled body. It leered, as if smiling and plotting. I brought my fist down and felt the crunch as its life blood oozed and mixed with the rain.

"Not on my world," I murmured and got back into my car.

Kissing Beetles
(a painful ode to an unfortunate allergy)

Brooke Mackenzie

Such an innocuous name, delightfully so
They get their tender name from their proclivity
to bite faces
Digging their snouts deep into the petal soft
skin of an eyelid
Or cheek as it blushes in sleep,
Leaving watery lumps behind as a morning
surprise
And they make my entire body blossom into
hives
Sprinkling that pollinated itch to the eyes and
lips and tongue
And when that happens
Air becomes scarce
And liquid luck in the shape of a needle
Is the only salvation for that unwelcome
penetration.

Their bites make me breathless
At night I feel the beetles crawling under my
skin
Scuttling across the fibers of my nerves
The mucus membranes of my skeletal system
Making toxic shapes in my limbs as they crawl
and zigzag,
Thick with chemical curiosity

Their little feet stinging with each step on the inside of my body where there is no relief

I think they might be in the couch

Or under the blanket as I battle my insomnia with the visual balm of television

But they're in me and so I start

Scratching, scratching, scratching

My fingernails can't reach

And the click clack clackety sound of their crawling

Echoes in the hollows of my bones and in the meaty space at the back of my jaw

And then the beetles find their way to my optic nerves

Where they tug and twist, master puppeteers

Forcing my eyelids open and my corneas to turn dry

And the bulge in my vision makes everything look convex

And the boiling blisters bubble up from a lower layer of my skin

Making my body crimson and my heart a deep plum purple

As it pumps air through swelling passages

And I thrash and scratch and scream and slowly fill with fluid

Drowning in my own body until finally,

Unsheathing my own EpiPen Excalibur,

I stab my villainous body in the thigh

The passageways open and the beetles disappear into puffs of smoke

Snaking out through my nostrils and my body heaves into breath

Tonight these unlikely foes have been vanquished

But they will be back

Too tempting is my taut skin and all my threaded fibers

The mincemeat parts of me…

The Invisible Spider That Flies in the Night

Dona Fox

First, a consciousness of a sort returned, then I realized I was naked and freezing. I tried to move, to sit up, but I was paralyzed, unable to send messages to my limbs.

Bright lights from above blinded me, but gradually the fog lifted and my vision cleared. Indeed, of all my senses vision seemed the sharpest—until it was as if I could see in all corners of the room at once. Gradually the minutest detail became clear.

I noted spiders had left beautiful traps in every corner of the room; their lacy web chains hung from the ceiling and swayed in imperceptible drafts.

The scent of a dirty ashtray drew me to look toward the man who stood beside the table I was lying on.

My gaze drifted down his sallow, unshaven cheeks. His surgical mask had slipped from his face.

Five of them hung over me; hooded, gowned— four of them were youthful with eager eyes above their masks. Ashtray-breath was not so young, though his eyebrows were still dark caterpillars, the lines that marked his years dug deep groves across his sagging face.

His fallen mask gave me a look straight up his nose; his nostrils were full of tiny black spiders and the small whitish balls that held their eggs.

He sniffed as he rubbed his nose with a gloved hand and some of the white disappeared - sucked into his brain, no doubt.

He mumbled words I couldn't understand, held out the same hand he'd wiped his nostrils with and someone else's hand, a smaller hand, slapped a shining blade into his open palm.

That's when I realized he was a surgeon. My surgeon.

The surgeon who bent over me as I stared up into his bloodshot pupils hadn't acknowledged me watching him. I feared the worst. He was high on 'something' and I was one of those horrible stories you read about-under anesthesia but awake.

Except in my case, I wasn't going to live to talk about my gruesome experience—about the surgery I hadn't wanted - the same surgery that killed my dad.

But my wife, Gina, and buddy Bobby talked me into it, made me feel guilty if I didn't have it, said I needed it if I wanted to be out of pain and enjoy watching my kids grow up.

So here I was in the operating room, freezing my butt off—just so I could be more active in my senior years. They didn't know the surgeon would be a living petri dish and high as a kite to boot.

The scalpel dove at me and I melted off the table to the floor. I was naked but my hospital gown was neatly folded on a shelf on the underside of the table. I bit it between my teeth.

I crawled helter-skelter like a giant four-legged spider dragging a hospital gown clenched between my teeth-until I arrived at the swinging double doors where I stood and took the chance of stopping for a quick glance over my shoulder.

I looked back at the four green gowned assistants waving their arms in the air as they ran around the body on the operating table. The drugged-up surgeon was nowhere in sight.

The surgery assistants were squawking now - once again their words were unintelligible to me. I felt sorry for the man on the table but there was no way I could help him and I surely didn't want to linger here.

I crawled under the double doors - careful—slow—looking back now and then to see if they'd heard a sound, if they'd noticed a change in the light or felt a bit of breeze from the hallway, but they were focused on the figure before them.

At first the floor was linoleum and the walls were battered at hip height from the passage of gurneys. I tried to slip into the hospital gown, thinking my only problem would be reaching behind to tie it, but it was worse than that—I must have been fuzzy-headed from the pre-surgery drugs for I seemed to have too many arms and legs and there was way too much cloth to sort out——so I discarded both the gown and my modesty as I ran.

I saw an escalator going up and I jumped on.

On the next floor natural light streamed in the windows. It was soon obvious I was running down a very long impersonal tan and cream carpeted hospital corridor - this was the public face of the hospital. To my right was a room filled with people, lounging. No - I felt their tension - they were anxiously waiting.

I scanned the room. There they were - my family. I sighed and scurried over to them.

"Let's get out of here," I said. "You won't believe what's going on down there. The OR is positively-" I stopped. The kids continued thumbing their phones, but that wasn't unusual.

My mother hadn't dropped a stitch on her knitting as she stared out the window—perhaps she hadn't heard me—she needed aids and refused to go in for a check-up. But Gina, my wife, whose hearing was perfect, was still doing her crossword puzzle; she hadn't even looked down at me. Yes, down at me. For some reason I felt very small as I stood on the floor between them.

"Can you hear me? Can't you see me!" I shouted; Gina scratched her ear in response.

Mom sighed and indicated her knitting - she had dropped a stitch.

The kids stretched and held out their empty palms.

I crawled up the leg onto a chair across from them and watched as Mom gave them money.

Gina's smile was soft as her lips moved, but I knew she was chiding my mother for spoiling our kids - why couldn't I hear what she was saying? Was it some after-effect of the drugs they'd given me for the surgery?

But why couldn't they see or hear me?

Mom nodded and said something.

Gina replied.

Then Mom most likely made a joke because she arched that one eyebrow of hers—a clever trick I'd spent hours in front of the mirror trying to duplicate.

My wife put her hands on her chest as if she were shocked at Mom's joke. They both laughed.

Mom wiped tears from her cheek; apparently her little joke made her sad.

Gina patted Mom's hand.

I jumped on the hem of Mom's skirt and ran up the folds. I'd sit in the cross formed by her knitting needles and get her attention.

Gina cried out in alarm.

Mom jumped up and dropped her knitting on the floor. They both brushed at Mom's skirt. I ran for my life.

I sheltered in a dark crevice under an empty chair, shaking. That was a close call. I needed to think, come up with a plan, something better than running up their legs.

Gina helped Mom pick up her knitting and they settled back into their chairs until a whoosh of air through the room must have got their attention as they both turned in their seats.

I ran up onto the arm of an empty chair to see what was going on. The new arrival was Bobby. I jumped up and down, waving my arms; surely, of all people, Bobby would see me.

Bobby had been my best friend since grade school. He brought the fresh air in with him as he stood in the doorway. Even at our age, in his throwback tight jeans and white tee, Bobby was magnificent. He made me feel old and useless as I

110

stood in the draft trying not to blow off the slick wooden arm of the chair.

He hugged Mom then he took Gina in his arms.

I felt a twinge of jealousy as he whispered something under her hair into her ear. Then he sat down beside my wife. Alarms were going off in my head. There was something wrong. Something I needed to tell Mom and Gina about Bobby. Something in him had changed. They weren't safe around him. But they couldn't hear me.

Bobby took Gina's hand and squeezed it, then he leaned toward the kids, all sincere and eager to please. Their faces lit up and Bobby pulled out the little pencil and notepad he was famous for. I ran up the wall to the ceiling and built a chain down so I could look over his shoulder. Hamburgers. My kids were so easy.

No problem. Let Bobby go get them hamburgers; meanwhile, I'd try to remember what was bothering me about him. I'd try to figure out a way to get my family to see me, to hear me. This would give me some time.

They waved him off with smiles - he made as if he was leaving, as if he was gone, in fact.

Then Gina pointed across the hall at the restroom. Mom nodded.

The kids went back to their phone and Mom to her knitting.

But Bobby hadn't left like everyone seemed to think. He lurked outside the restroom waiting for Gina.

No one else saw Gina go with him.

No one but me saw her leave with him.

He planned it so no one would know where she was.

I couldn't let that happen. I couldn't let my wife get into that old windowless utility van with Bobby. We'd joked about it, called it a creeper van. It wasn't so funny now that my wife was stepping into the drab old van with him.

And then I remembered the big lock on Bobby's basement. It appeared after his parents died and the house was all his—his alone to do as he wanted. I was his best friend and he wouldn't let me go down there.

I ran after them. The air at the doorway hit me like a cement wall; I felt the invisible damp barrier from side to side, up and down. I backed up and tried again. Umph.

"Hey! What's the deal here?" I looked at the receptionist, "why can't I get out this door?"

She ignored me. I watched helplessly as my wife climbed into Bobby's creeper van and he shut the door. He looked back at the hospital and I swear he smirked at me.

It was the smirk that did it.

I ran past the lounge where my family waited for my surgery to be over and jumped on the escalator.

The addict doctor had changed into his street clothes and came out of his office, car keys in hand. He was so fried he had to hold the wall as he headed for the door that read <u>Doctor's Parking Garage</u>.

I flew up his nose as he snorted the last bits of white dust.

112

His mind was a weird, confused place but weak and tired. I took over quite easily, glad that I was driving and not him.

I was tripping all the way to Bobby's place, having a kind of double image where the second picture is slightly off-skew from the first. Almost like a double-vision of the same route, except it was recollections instead of sight.

I recalled other trips to Bobby's house and meetings with Bobby where I was not present. Was I tripping on the good doctor's drugs? Before we even arrived, I remembered going down into Bobby's basement - a place I'd never been so these were the doctor's memories. In these strange shadow memories, I watched Bobby handing over money, a lot of money.

And now, for real, I'm there, in the basement. There's Bobby and here's my wife - is she asleep or dead? No, she's not dead. Thankfully, she's breathing.

"I've got a live one this time, Doc. Lots of parts. What's she worth?" Bobby said.

I was about to jump on him, tear his vile throat out when the cops burst in. They'd been on to the doctor and Bobby for a while. Bobby and the doctor had kind of a symbiotic thing going. The doctor needed money for his coke habit. Bobby was a serial killer who got rid of the bodies by selling the parts to the doctor and various others. Some in professions too hideous to name here, others that would simply shock and revolt you to no good purpose.

The arrests happened fast. I like to believe I am an unsung hero of this story because there's no way the doc would have made it to Bobby's house that day if I hadn't been driving. I played a big part in helping months of investigation come together. Though I got to say I kind of resent they let the doc wield his scalpel over me and even let Bobby take my wife into his basement.

The doctor was processed and now he was stretched out on a cot in the prison's medical unit in a cold jail cell. I left the way I'd entered him, right through his mushy brain and out his hairy nostrils.

I crawled across his face and stared into the doctor's dilated pupils, wondering how long it was going to take before he crashed to earth. It was time to leave him in the cell where he belonged and head out in search of my family.

But whose body shall I enter to return to my family? I sent out my hairy little feelers. Touching the bodies in the prison softly here and there. Sliding down a sleeping cheekbone, hiding under covers in the dark. Slipping up a drain spout. Certainly not the prisoners—that won't get me out—and I don't fancy being in law enforcement.

Ah, but I sense a presence with me on the cold page as I try to move, to sit up - to flee. I'm practically invisible, leaving a slight tickle in the ear as the story ends and consciousness of a sort returns.

Sinkhole

Tom Leaf

It was raining the day the sinkhole opened up, fat greasy rain, the kind that don't let up so your shirt sticks to your stomach like a second skin and you can't tell if it's water or snot running off the end of your nose.

'You seen it?'

Charlie had to shout, because of the rain and on account of his being deaf in one ear. 'Seen what?'

'Sinkhole, big as hell, right up in our top field. Happened last night, I reckon.'

We chugged up in there in Charlie's shitty pick-up, rain hammering off the roof like a tin of nails, stupid ass wipers squeaking and flopping and making not a bit of difference. The sinkhole was big, at least thirty feet across, the rim of it all ragged with corn hanging limp down over fresh black dirt.

Charlie stood a few feet back from the edge, grey hair plastered to his forehead, looking smug as if he'd dug the fucking thing himself.

'Well, what do you think?'

'It's a sinkhole.' I said, 'not a lot else to say.'

'Seems pretty deep to me.' Charlie said, craning his scrawny neck forward. 'Can't see the bottom of it.'

He paused as if working out a real hard math problem.

'Hey, we could get rid of stuff in it,' Charlie said. 'Dump off a load of crap. Put the word out, let folks know we got ourselves a free for all. Make a quick buck.'

'Ain't a free for all if you're gonna charge people.'

***

The three of us went back later that day. Charlie brought his boy along to help, except Cody was dumber than a rock and didn't know his ass from no sinkhole; anyhow we went back up there, Charlie's truck groaning under the weight of all the junk we'd collected.

'What's in them barrels, Pa?' Cody said, squinting at the faded labels with his one good eye.

'Ain't none of your concern, boy, just get 'em shifted.'

'Kinda looks like army lettering on the side of those barrels, Charlie.' I said.

'Not a clue, buckaroo. They been rustin' out in the long grass behind the barn for as long as we been there. Christ, I'm pretty sure they was there even before my Granddaddy worked the farm. Sure ain't anything to worry about – hell, I can remember Cody playing all over them when he was shorter than shit.'

We bounced the barrels off the truck quick as you like and Cody rolled them to the edge of the sinkhole, laughing and hollering like a circus monkey.

116

The barrels got rolled in along with a crap load of tyres, two stained mattresses and a spongy timber sideboard all swollen with mould, its drawers hanging out like brown tongues. The stuff disappeared down the sinkhole slicker than spit.

'We got ourselves a money maker.' Charlie said with a tobacco stained grin.

***

Charlie spread the word, and soon enough there was a steady stream of folks wanting to dump their crap. Cody made a sign - *five bucks a truck* - all painted up in red letters and Charlie even took to selling bottles of lukewarm beer from the back of his pick-up to those folks waiting their turn in the queue.

'I ain't got to worry about getting a fine of the planet huggers, neither,' said Charlie 'on account of the fact that Sheriff Dawes himself was up here only yesterday dropping off some old asbestos sheets from a lean-to he's been breaking up. I didn't ask him for the five bucks and he didn't offer it. He said to call it our business arrangement.'

For four days straight, the townspeople unloaded their crap down the sinkhole, everything from broken TV's, waste oil, sacks of dirty diapers, broken lawn furniture, car parts and animal carcasses.

'What the hell, Kevin? How come you got a truckload of dead cows?'

'Couldn't keep up with the vet payments. Lost some of the herd to mastitis. Their titties got rotten, so I had to shoot 'em.'

'Get 'em in the hole, Kevin, they're starting to stink.'

***

The sinkhole must have been deep. No-one ventured right up to the edge, on account of how loose the earth was there and so everything had to be rolled or thrown in from a little ways off and yet no matter how many truckloads of stuff got hauled into the sinkhole, the top of the growing junk pile couldn't be seen. On the afternoon of the fifth day, the queue had started to die down and Charlie had gotten bored dishing out warm beer to the locals.

'Time to call it a day, Cody – we made our money and I can't stand the stink coming out of the pit anymore.

'What now, Pa? How we gonna fill it in?'

'We ain't. Let it be, that's the plan. Eventually the sides will fall in.'

Cody yanked the hand painted sign off the fence post and flicked it over the edge of the sinkhole.

'Gotta be deeper than the Devil's ass, Pa.'

Cody was leaning towards the edge, looking back at us and cupping his scrawny hand to his ear.

'Still can't hear no bump from the bottom.'

To this day, I still got no idea what the fuck it was that took him. All I can remember, apart from the screaming and the way Cody's feet slid about

118

like he was dancing right there at the edge, was what looked like a spider's leg, but longer than a tree, thick and black, with more knuckle joints than you could count, unfolding itself out of that hole and stickin' him like a frankfurter and draggin' him screaming and coughing, his face all red and wet, dragging him back down, down and away and out of sight. Charlie was hollering for help, but we was way out of hearing distance of anyone else so he was wasting his breath and I was just stood there, struck dumb with shock. Cody's screams could be heard getting fainter and fainter until they got cut off real quick. Charlie ran towards the edge of the sinkhole eyes wide with terror, then he dropped to his knees. He fell forwards, crawling on his stomach, like a commando, calling out his son's name over and over, with me shouting at him to come back, to come away from the edge. Something else come out of the sinkhole then, but it weren't that spider leg or whatever the fuck the thing had been that took Cody. It was an arm, like a man's arm but different. No bones in it, just a long tube, all grey and flexible with a big bendy hand on the end of it snaking across the corn and grabbing Charlie by his collar. I was that close I could see there weren't no nails on its fingers, just blobby ends like the kind a frog has. Charlie held his breath and he was looking back, staring straight into my face, his mouth all wide open but no sound coming out. A thorny stick thing was pushing out from the back of the hand, getting all long and stretchy and then it pushed at the back of Charlie's head and then made a sort of snap noise as it kept on pushing into his skull. I seen Charlie's eyes roll back so no pupils was showing and his whole body started twitching like he was fitting or something like that. He went limp and the arm began sliding back, but this time it was pulling Charlie with it. He didn't make no sound and all I could hear was the drag of his boots across the corn. He got pulled over the edge of the sinkhole and that was the last I seen of Charlie Bannon.

***

No-one's been back to the top field lately. Folks have talked about filling in the sinkhole but there isn't anyone with balls big enough to go up there. I went near the place the other night a little tight with booze, so I guess my curiosity had gotten the better of me. The moon was fat and low over the top field, everything all lit up silvery an' that. Never went near the edge, too scared for that, just stood there, listening. There was a breeze rustling through the corn but that was it. No night birds or fox sounds, or nothing. I got squirrely on account of how quiet it was so I was going back the way I came and I heard a real low moan like a cow makes when it's pushing out a calf. I ran out of there, got in my truck and that was that. Definitely locked my door that night. Other folks keep talking about getting some dynamite from the Hendricks' quarry and blowin' the shit out of the sinkhole. But they ain't yet and probably won't.

***

Been rumours that a second sinkhole's opened up over Richmond way. Hope they're better prepared than we was.

Rejection

Thomas M. Malafarina

"We all learn lessons in life. Some stick, some don't. I have always learned more from rejection and failure than from acceptance and success." - *Henry Rollins*

"I really wish I was less of a thinking man and more of a fool not afraid of rejection." - *Billy Joel*

"Sometimes I feel my whole life has been one big rejection." - *Marilyn Monroe*

"Most fears of rejection rest on the desire for approval from other people. Don't base your self-esteem on their opinions." - *Harvey Mackay*

Becky's eyes fluttered open as she slowly crawled her way out of the darkness back to the world of consciousness. She woke with her head hanging down, her chin on her chest, and a steady stream of rapidly cooling drool dripping off her chin. As her vision cleared, she could see her legs; her naked legs, but couldn't seem to grasp the significance of what she was seeing.

The room around her was dark, save for a few candles burning on a nearby dresser. It was one of those tall five-drawer dressers her grandmother used to call a... what was it? A big boy? No, it was a high boy. Although the flickering light was minimal, it was bright enough for Becky to recognize the dresser had seen better days. It was scared, faded, and its remaining paint was chipping and peeling. The wood was split in places and one of the drawers hung askew. The soles of her feet were cold as if they were resting against a concrete floor. Likewise, the air around her was cool and damp. She was certain she was in a basement. Across the room, thick curtains were hanging over a tiny window up near the open-beamed ceiling. The window was visible only as a sliver where the curtains met. She could tell it was almost sunset outside. Once again she noticed the room's dank, musty odor much more strongly now realizing it was the stench of decay. There was also the faint aroma of the melting candle wax and a sulfur-tinged burning that made her wonder strangely for a moment, why the candles weren't scented. That certainly would have improved things. She realized that was an odd thought for her to have in such a confusing situation.

Becky found she was unable to focus. She felt peculiar as if she were coming down from some sort of anesthetic. Dreamlike surrealism seemed to engulf her. Then she noticed discomfort in her back and realized something was wrong. She seemed to be sitting upright in a wooden chair of some sort. As she edged closer to consciousness, she was able to sense her flesh pressing against the chair's hard smooth, and cold wooden surface. When she tried to lift her arms, Becky looked down and saw they both had been duct-taped to the arms of the heavy chair.

As she tried to move her feet, she felt her ankles were likewise bound to the chair. Panicking, Becky tried to rock the chair first front-to-back then left-to-right, but her attempts were useless. It became obvious that in addition to the chair being heavy, it was fastened somehow securely to the floor. Perhaps it was cemented or bolted in place. Whatever the case, the thing wouldn't budge.

Now completely awake, Becky did a quick inventory of herself to see just what sort of trouble she was in. With relief, she saw she was not completely naked and still wore her bra and panties. However, the relief was short-lived. Someone had brought her to this place, wherever this place was, had removed her clothes and secured her in this chair. But for what reason, and perhaps more importantly, to what eventual purpose? Becky decided her best chance was to go on the offensive and do her best not to show the fear she felt inside. She shouted into the darkness, "What the Hell is this? Who are you? I demand to know what this is all about!"

A chair scraped somewhere in a shadowed corner of the room as its inhabitant stood and slowly came into view. He was a gaunt young man in his late twenties with long, dark, greasy black hair and more tattoos and piercings than she had ever seen on one person before. He wore a filthy, yellowed wife-beater tee-shirt and equally dirty and faded jeans. Strangely, his feet were clad in a new, clean pair of florescent pink Crocs. He stared at Becky through dark haunted raccoon eyes as his mouth hung agape in a hang-dog expression. There was a rank, unwashed odor about him and when he spoke, his breath was as foul as a sewer.

"Hello, Becky. I've been waiting for you to wake up. You reacted poorly to the drug I used to bring you here. For a while, I thought you might be dead. That would have been bad." He smiled what would have been a big, toothy grin had it not been for his twisted collection of brown and rotten teeth looking like broken tombstones in an ancient cemetery.

Becky stared at the man's soiled, filthy and unshaven, face and saw something crawling from the frayed top of his tee-shirt and up along his neck. It was a tiny spider. She loathed spiders. It didn't matter how small or unthreatening the thing might be, she was terrified of all spiders. She couldn't recall the origin of her arachnophobia but suspected it must have formed at a very early age, because for as long as she could remember it had been her greatest of fears.

The young man lifted his hand and plucked the spider from his grime-covered neck and stared closely at it for a few seconds. For a moment, Becky was certain the man would either crush the spider in his fingers or put the wriggling thing into his mouth and eat it alive. Because that was the sort of thing crazy people did, and it was obvious that this wretched creature standing before her was as insane as someone could be. To make matters worse, She was his helpless prisoner. Then he slowly held the spider out to her, putting the twitching arachnid an inch from her face. It took everything Becky had not to scream in terror as its legs wiggled in front of her.

Her captor said in a calm and disturbingly normal voice, "I've done my research as all good authors should and learned that you have a terrible fear of spiders, Becky. Is that true? I was amazed to learn it because here you are, running a successful publishing company, yet you're terrified of these tiny creatures. This is the same woman who decides on a daily, whose stories are good enough to publish, and who gets rejected. I mean seriously Becky, you could crush one of these tiny creatures in your hands as easily as you crush the dreams and spirits of young writers hoping for a break."

With that, the young man did crush the spider between his dirty fingers. When he did, liquid shot forward and splattered Becky's creek. Struggling to turn her face away from both the remains of the spider as well as the man's rank breath, Becky managed to demand, "Who are you? How do you know me? Why am I here?"

"Questions, questions. So many questions. You truly are the curious sort aren't you, Becky my dear," the man said as he flicked the crushed spider off his fingers and onto Becky's leg.

"Oh please no. Jesus no. Please take it off me," Becky cried in terror as all the bravado she had managed to muster vanished.

"Relax. Relax." The man said as he flicked the spider carcass with his finger, sending it flying across the room into the shadows. Becky was still staring down at her leg and every muscle in her body was tense, "Please, please get that too."

126

The man looked a bit confused for a moment until he noticed one of the spider's legs still laying on Becky's naked thigh. "Ok, ok I'll get it. Wow! You certainly do have some serious issues with our little spider-friends, don't you?" He picked off the leg, held it between his fingers, which still bore the residual goo from the crushed spider, and brushed it gently across Becky's clenched and trembling lips.

Her terror came out as a high-pitched keening, which emanated from her nose and throat, sounding like the whimpering on a wounded kitten. Her eyes were held tightly shut as tears streamed down her cheeks. When at last she no longer felt the leg brushing her lips and she heard the sound of her captor stepping away she unclenched her lips and opened her eyes. The young man was standing a few feet in front of her, grinning his rotten-toothed grin.

"God, how I enjoyed that!"

Becky was on the verge of hysteria. She pleaded, "Why... why are you... are you doing this to me? I don't know... who you are. Please... Please...""That's right, Becky my dear. You don't know who I am. And thanks to you and people like you, no one knows who I am. But you don't care about that, do you? For you, it's just another day at the office, running your horror publishing business. You're the queen at Terror Tales Publishing, aren't you? You're the Lord High Muckity-muck of your industry. You read a submission wave your magic wand or royal scepter and decide yea or nay. Isn't that right, Becky? To you, it's all just words on a page, subject to whatever mood you happen to be in on any particular day. You never take the time to think about what effect your rejection might have on a struggling author like me."

"You... you're an author?" she asked, struggling desperately to try to make some sense out of something so senseless.

"Oh yes, I most certainly am. And apparently, I seem to be one of your favorite targets for rejection."

"Look, I'm sorry... but I'm afraid I don't know you or what I've done to upset you." "Horror in Paradise." The man said.

Becky was confused, "What? I don't understand."

The man was becoming agitated and started rattling off what at first Becky thought were unrelated phrases, getting louder and angrier with each utterance, "Horror In Paradise! I Eat Your Young! Death At Daycare! Incestual Terror!" That last one especially triggered a faint memory. Incestual Terror? What was that? Then it all started to come into focus. All those phrases were short story titles. She had heard them all before. Hell, she had read and rejected them all before. Then a name popped into her mind.

She looked at the young man and whispered knowingly, "Artimus Dread?"

"Ah yes. So, you do remember." He replied.

Becky remembered very well, "The pseudonym – she was sure it was a pseudonym – Artimus Dread was an author who had submitted dozens of short stories to her publishing company. And she had rejected every one of them and for good reasons.

128

Not only was the writing amateurish at best, the grammar ridiculous, and the spelling atrocious, but the moron never once even attempted to her submission guidelines. As if that weren't bad enough, the subject matter of his stories was not only in violation of her publishing company policy but went against even the lowest of moral codes, as the story titles alone suggested. When she received the first story, "Horror In Paradise" she was a bit curious even though it was obvious from the first sentence that the story was going to be garbage. She could still recall that first line of the story. It seemed to haunt her like a hated tune that got stuck in her head. She recalled the ridiculous opening line, "Although they were stranded on a beautiful island paradise, their sexual and cannibalistic urges would soon turn it into a Hell on earth."

Becky looked at her captor and said, "You."

"Yes me, Becky. How many of my stories did you reject? A dozen? Two dozen? Maybe more. In the beginning, you would simply send a generic email reply saying something like, 'We're sorry but we have to pass on this at this time. Good luck placing it elsewhere.' But eventually, that wasn't enough, was it? After a while, you had to start adding your editorial comments to my rejections, comments like 'juvenile, sophomoric, embarrassing' to name a few. And as if that weren't bad enough you had to step up your game with words like, 'sick, twisted and warped.' Nice move, Becky real nice."

"Look… I'm… I'm sorry…"

"Shut up, you insolent ignorant bitch! I'm the one in charge now! I'm the new Lord High Muckity-muck! I'm the editor in this story!" He screamed at the top of his lungs.

He stood in front of her panting like a dog for a few moments, trying desperately to regain some sort of composure. He had a plan for this woman, and he couldn't allow his anger to cause him to do something to change that plan. True, she would end up dead either way, but the plan was a much more suitable path to follow.

He released a deep stinking breath and said calmly, "I especially recall the last rejection email you sent. That one was for 'Incestual Terror'. You said, and I quote, 'You are one of the sickest bastards I have ever encountered. You should quit writing, crawl back into whatever primordial sludge you crawled out of, and do us all a favor by curling up and dying.' Becky, oh my sweet Becky. That was not very nice of you now, was it? You of all people should know to stick to the standard, polite and generic rejection letter format. A publisher should never offer such a blatant criticism of an author's work. If so, such a publisher might find herself in a situation she can't handle, like this one."

"What... what do you want from me?" Becky pleaded.

The young man smiled his hideous grin and said, "Want? What do I want? Why Becky, I thought someone as smart as you claim to be would have already figured that out by now. I want you to die. And I want you to die slowly, painfully and to lose your mind before death finally comes to claim you."

"No… please… I'm sorry. I truly am. Look, I'll make a deal with you. Let me go… and I promise I'll publish your stories. I'll even do an entire book of your work. You… you won't have to share the pages with anyone. It will be all yours."

"Too much, too little, too late as the song goes, Becky. There's no need for you to compromise your precious literary integrity. I'm already in the process of self-publishing on one of the many websites available, so, as you can see, I am no longer in need of your services."

Becky said, "But what about promotion? I… I could help promote your work if you did it through our company."

"Sorry, Sweetie. That ship has sailed for you, I'm afraid. Now, give me a second or two to get ready, then I'll be saying goodbye… forever."

Becky watched in terror as the young man walked over to one end of the room and pulled out a video camera on a tripod. He must have stolen it somewhere because it was obvious he could never have afforded such a camera. He pointed the lens at her, and she could see her focusing it to get the right image.

He said, "I could use my cell phone for this, but to do so I would have to stay here in the room with you and that wouldn't be good for me. The special treat I have in store for you is not something I wouldn't want to be part of for my health and wellbeing. I'll return eventually when I render this room safe again, that is after you're dead."

"What… what are you going to do to me?"

"Oh, you'll see very soon, sweet Becky."

The man walked over to the shadowy area to the right of the tripod and slid a two-foot square wooden crate over into the light. He looked at Becky and gave that decayed jack-o-lantern grin one last time. He pulled off the lid of the crate and quickly backed away into the shadows. Becky heard the slamming of a door and knew her captor was gone. She was alone... with whatever was inside the box.

She stared at the black opening of the crate waiting with dread anticipation of what might be inside. She believed she knew, but hoped against all hope that she was wrong. She was not wrong. Within a few seconds, she saw something hook itself over the top of the box. It was thin, black, and hairy. She immediately recognized it as a leg... a huge spider's leg. Soon other legs made their way out of the box followed by furry bodies of several other large arachnids. Then the smaller ones came, skittering over the backs of the larger ones. Then the jumpers; horrid little things that jumped down to the floor with ease. There were dozens of the wretched creatures, no hundreds. Like a flood of legs and fur-covered bodies, the spiders kept coming. Becky's breath caught in her throat. She wanted to scream, had to scream but couldn't find the air to do so. She realized with horror that there were thousands of spiders. Most of them were scurrying to the darker, shadowed areas of the room, but far too many were crawling toward her.

When she felt the first spider creeping onto her foot, Becky was uncertain whether it had been real or if perhaps her fear-stimulated brain had imagined the sensation. As terror raced through her with the speed of a bullet, Becky decided not to look down. If she didn't see the creature, maybe she could convince herself these phantom sensations were nothingness than her vivid imagination working overtime. She had just about convinced herself when she felt a second one, then a third. Soon her feet and ankles were awash with the feeling of hundreds of tiny legs crawling about her feet and working their way up her ankles.

Reluctantly, Becky opened her eyes just as several spiders made their way over her knees and up onto her thighs. She shook her legs as best as she was able, screaming, crying, and thrashing trying her best to shake the horrible things off her legs. That was when she felt the first stinging bite, which sent a red-hot flame into the meat of her thigh. Then she felt another and another. Too late she realized her thrashing had done nothing but agitate the creatures and cause them to attack her.

She sat trembling, too terrified to try to shake them off any longer, the spiders continued to crawl up past her thighs and onto her bare stomach. She could feel the hundreds of tiny insectile feet scurrying up her belly and onto her breasts. Becky began to feel strange. Her legs had become numb and her thoughts were becoming confused as if she were falling asleep. She felt several additional hot stings on her stomach and upper chest.

Becky had stopped crying. She had stopped panicking. As if accepting her fate, or perhaps it was the result of the quantities of spider venom in her system, she calmly sat as the spiders did their work. Maybe it wasn't the toxins that had caused this. Perhaps her captor was right and she had lost her sanity. She supposed that was a possibility since no sane person could sit still while hundreds of spiders covered her body and continued to sting and bite her repeatedly. Now they were crawling up her neck and over her chin, trying desperately to get between her tightly clenched lips. Several smaller spiders crawled up into her nostrils. Becky sneezed involuntarily her body reacting to the tickling sensation inside her nose. But soon enough creatures had blocked her nostrils that she was no longer able to breathe. She knew what would happen if she allowed her mouth to open, but had no choice. She opened wide and took what would be her last cleansing breath and could feel hundreds of tiny, shuffling feet crawl over her lips, filling her mouth and slithering down her throat. She knew this was the end. Her last thought iconically was that some people don't handle rejection very well.

Sang-Froid

Liam A. Spinage

They don't tell you about the cold. They don't need to. Everyone knows it's cold. Anyway, it's not the measurements of the thermometer that are important. Not to people, anyway. It's what the cold *does* to you that matters.

Franklin stands patiently on the deck, looking out across a sea of white. No speck of foliage to break the monotony. No promontory of grey stone to act as a landmark, just an endless sea of pack ice.

They don't tell you about the silence either. No birdsong, No insects. The reason they don't tell you is that it isn't silent. The pack ice itself fills in the gaps that the rest of nature has left absent. It howls, it sizzles, it cracks, it yowls and screams; it is thunder, it is driving rain, it is the beating sun for a land and a sea that knows none of these things.

It is because of this ice that their ship, the Erebus, is trapped; their very mission under threat. A deadly labyrinth of shifting floes, cracking and reforming. He knows now that the glory will not be his. He knows the price he must pay for his folly.

Franklin is haunted. By his own ambition, by the imperial hubris of the former captain and his botanist. But most of all by the tiny spider-like creatures they discovered in the hold. Creatures the Erebus must have picked up on its former voyage -

a voyage to Antarctica, about as far away from their current location as is humanly possible.

These guests are so tiny they are near-invisible, even before you take into account they are translucent as if fashioned from the very ice itself. They are clearly possessed of a singular collective mind of some sort which would fascinate any gentleman scientist. An intelligence to match the brain of any respected philosopher: a persistent constitution enough to match that of the most stalwart explorer. They have devastated the hold supplies. They have spewed forth across his body, burying themselves within his clothing and within the very folds of his flesh, deeper, deeper, deeper until they find blood.

His blood coagulates on the slightest wound, like the shaving cut he accidentally delivered yesterday. It freezes on contact with the air, flecks of ice glistening on his skin while the tiny spiders run over and under his skin, working their way through his flesh and his resolve in equal measure.

For days now, the howls of these minute monstrosities have dug themselves into his mind, permeating the very core of his being. Yet he persists. He stands stoically, sucking on his pipe, staring across the never-ending bleakness of his world, which fascinates and horrifies in equal measure.

Franklin knows the time has come. He will not be marked by his failure, but by his strength. His cold, rational decisions. When he acts, he knows that it will save his crew - for now, at least. He reaches into the greatcoat and digs out his journal, glancing over it as if it were an object foreign to him now. He must record his decision. His crew must never know what he is about to do - or why - lest they mark themselves unwillingly as prey for the crawling chaos that plays out under his skin. But others must know. Will know. When it is found, there will be lectures given in the (natural societies) about its contents and their meaning. Those things man was not meant to know will be known. There is so much they still do not understand, and will not until science has advanced to the point where these things can be studied, calculated, prevented...

And until humanity has understood that they are not alone. That these tiny minds are, in concert, equal to ours and just as unthinking, conquering, blindly malevolent in their actions.

It is a matter of honour. It is a matter of sacrifice.

Franklin edges forward. One moment - a singular fraction of hesitation in a mind ridden with desperation and resolve alike.

"And now, we commit this body to the deep..."

Splash.

Big Dolly

Tom Leaf

Walsh glared at Colin.

'According to this here letter, Boulton reckons you're a handy fellow to have on board.'

Colin nodded meekly, eyes lowered, unwilling to meet Walsh's interrogating stare.

'But, he also writes here that you and him had a falling out over his missus. Reckons you're a peeping tom. That true?'

Another nod.

'No women here, just me and the potatoes. The potatoes go in the sack. The sack goes in the trolley. When the trolley is full of sacks, you wheel the trolley to the barn. Understood?'

Another nod from Colin.

'Feeble minded or not, I'll smack you shitless if you don't pull your weight, got it?'

Colin gulped, licking excess spittle from the corners of his thin lips.

He got it.

'Now, listen, I ain't got enough money to pay you, but you'll get fed and you can sleep in the barn.'

***

As summer limped into autumn, Colin spent long, solitary days in the top field, scrabbling potatoes into scratchy sacks. The lane leading back to the barn was deeply rutted and Colin, teeth gritted in effort, would curse Walsh's wooden trolley under his breath.

'I swear the bastard thing's got square wheels.'

The potatoes come out covered in black, wet earth but Colin didn't mind. After a while he became used to the smell of the earth, the smell of the scratchy damp sacks and the smell of his own pale, unwashed skin.

There was no running water in the barn.

Colin scavenged a tin bucket from amongst the thick nettles sprawled behind the barn, furtively filling it with brackish water from the standpipe next to the farmhouse. At the back of the barn, where the shadows were thickest, he'd wound himself a nest amongst cobwebbed sacks and clawed out a toilet hole from a patch of bare earth.

'Shittin' in the dirt like a bloody fox. What would Mother say?' he whispered to himself. Colin would occasionally think about his mother. Two days before his third birthday, Colin's mother had left him on a park bench and told him to wait. She never returned to collect him. He often had a dream where his mother was making him a sandwich. In the dream, she was always naked.

Colin did his best to keep out of the way of Walsh, for Walsh drank heavily and most nights Colin would lie huddled in the barn listening to the man dashing any object within easy reach to the flagstone floor in furious rage, his terrible roars thundering through the squat farmhouse.

There were evenings when Walsh would remain sober just long enough to leave Colin a slab of cold gammon or half a stale loaf on the farmhouse wall.

Usually, however, the wall would be empty and Colin would curl up in his nest of sacks gnawing on a raw potato, knowing that he would regret it the following morning, squatting over his earth toilet, racked with pain.

***

On Tuesday, Colin's loneliness became too much too bear.

On Wednesday, in the top field, far away from prying eyes, Colin made Big Dolly.

Big Dolly's sackcloth body was rough and between its right leg and its left leg there was a crease where Colin could hide his winky. Big Dolly's tin bucket of a head was smooth and hard with a rusted split of a mouth and a blood painted smile. Scavenged rabbit teeth rattled around inside Big Dolly's hollow head like tiny dice.

Colin really fancied Big Dolly.

Thursday night, he decided to move Big Dolly into the barn. The squeak of the wheels echoed off the stone farmhouse walls as he trundled the wooden trolley across the moonlit farmyard. Colin was not concerned by this as no gammon had been left on the wall. Walsh was shitfaced and dead to the world.

Colin lay down amongst the sacks, curled into an unlikely shape and immediately fell into a deep, fitful sleep, mumbling incoherently while strange dreams whirled inside his peculiar mind.

Big Dolly, not asleep, remained propped up in the corner staring at nothing through yellow felt-pen eyes.

***

Dawn broke and Colin was woken by a voice he didn't recognise.

Big Dolly wanted his attention.

'Get up.' Big Dolly whispered, 'go out, go down to the village and see what you can find.'

The path to the village crossed a large field, damp with morning dew. Colin liked how soft the dew felt on his dirty, bare feet and how hard the handle of the scythe felt in his dirty, bare hand. He soon found a cottage with a family inside. When the family saw Colin, their mouths and eyes opened wide. After the wet work was done, Colin stacked their bodies in the earthy cellar of their cottage then wheeled Big Dolly, hidden under a ragged tarpaulin, from Walsh's barn and down into the depths of the empty cottage.

'A better place for us to hide.' he thought.

Colin told Big Dolly about the family and the things he had done to them.

He whispered into Big Dolly's hard, blood painted face and he touched Big Dolly's rough sackcloth body.

Big Dolly listened to every one of his mumbled prayers and forgave him.

The next morning, before the sun rose, Colin left the cellar and went looking for another family.

The man of the family escaped but Colin found him hiding in a lane. He had made his face all wet and runny with sad tears and one of his pyjama legs was torn.

'Don't cry, Mister.' Colin said, wiping away the man's tears with the curved edge of the scythe.

Colin had now collected two families.

'Well done.' whispered Big Dolly.

'I'm a busy boy.' Colin said.

'Yes, you are. Keep going.'

***

On the third morning, just before sunrise, Colin helped a small blond boy. Helped him out of his bedroom window and into a sack. After he'd finished with the small blond boy, Colin showed Big Dolly his prize.

'Just the one this time.' Colin panted, his tongue thick with blood.

'Keep going.' said Big Dolly.

***

Colin spent that afternoon cross-legged on the cellar floor cleaning the scythe, occasionally pushing the cellar people with his fingers. They felt softer than the day before. Colin liked that.

As the feeble daylight creeping around the edge of the cellar hatch began to fade, Colin removed his trousers and lit a candle he had found. He wanted this night with Big Dolly to be special.

'Look, Big Dolly,' he said, gesturing towards the pile of cellar people, 'see how many I've found.'

Big Dolly lay slumped, lumpy cloth legs draped over the pile of people. Big Dolly didn't move. The ends of Big Dolly's arms and legs were tied with rope so the wet earth inside her floppy sackcloth body didn't slide out.

'Wake up, Big Dolly and look at my collection.'

Big Dolly's tin face, large as a moon, turned creakily towards Colin, voice shrill, words coming out stretched like elastic bands.

'Not enough things. Find more.'

Colin stared into Big Dolly's yellow eyes, scared by what he saw there.

'Don't stop now,' Big Dolly hissed, 'busy boys never stop.'

***

The old woman died easily; her barking dog put up a fight.

Colin, his arm throbbing with bite marks, laid out what was left of the two bodies alongside the others.

'More cellar people.' Colin whispered, his pale grey eyes avoiding Big Dolly's unblinking stare. Big Dolly said nothing. Big Dolly's sackcloth legs had soaked up blood from the people pile and were turning pink. Colin leant forward to move them.

'Don't touch me.' Big Dolly growled. Colin paused, eyes wide with fear.

Big Dolly sat up, tin face wobbling on its cloth neck.

'More. Collect more.'

Colin ran from the cellar on shaking legs, spending that afternoon huddled in the woodshed.

***

On the fifth morning, as the sun crept over the edge of the world, Colin collected three more. A young couple, new to the village and their mewling baby. Hacked and stacked in the cellar. Nice and neat. Colin was exhausted and his t-shirt, limp with blood, clung to his concave stomach like a second skin. Big Dolly slowly stood up and, swaying on stained cloth legs, swung a handless arm at the pile on the cellar floor.

'More. Now.'

Big Dolly lurched towards Colin, tin head lolling back and forth.

'More.'

'Please, Big Dolly. I want to go to sleep.'

Big Dolly lumbered up against Colin, lopsided. The rope that tied the bottom of her left leg had come undone and dark, wet soil, thick with spiders, spilled out. Inside the bucket face, rabbit teeth bounced and rattled against the mouth split, frantic and hungry.

'No. More. Sleep.' bellowed Big Dolly.

She bent backwards, bulbous body folded in half at the waist.

144

The spiders freed from the soil were everywhere, their fat glistening bodies scuttling across the entirety of Big Dolly's blood soaked sackcloth legs.

Big Dolly snapped back upright, butting Colin with a tin bucket smack.

Colin dropped like a felled ox, nose broken, howling in pain.

The spiders, in a single movement, scrambled away from Big Dolly, racing towards Colin's open mouth, determined to nest inside his wet, pink hole.

Colin scrabbled on hands and knees towards the cellar stairs, pursued by the army of spiders, insistent and hungry, while Big Dolly loomed ever nearer, dragging its flaccid left leg. Colin reached the bottom tread and, digging in with splintered fingernails, began to claw his way up, tread by tread, eyes wide with fear. The timber stairs, rotten with age, split in half, Colin fell face forward onto the cellar floor and the horde of spiders swarmed over him, a river of hungry, skittering death swamping his flailing body completely.

Big Dolly issued a final triumphant howl of victory and fell forward, its swollen body bursting on impact, burying Colin under a mass of clumped dirt and blood soaked sackcloth.

***

Calls from worried relatives and the subsequent police search of the village led to the discovery of the fourteen mutilated carcasses in the cellar. As horrific as the discoveries were, the cause of death in each case was apparent.

What remained of Colin, however, was more puzzling. The body cavity was swaddled in sackcloth and crammed with soil, the skull full to the brim with spiders' eggs and a crescent of rabbit teeth arranged, with great care, on top of his slack, dead lips as if imparting a final, forlorn kiss.

Meet the Authors

Ed Ahern resumed writing after forty odd years in foreign intelligence and international sales. He's had over three hundred stories and poems published so far, and six books. Ed works the other side of writing at Bewildering Stories, where he sits on the review board and manages a posse of six review editors.

https://www.twitter.com/bottomstripper
https://www.facebook.com/EdAhern73/?ref=bookm arks
https://www.instagram.com/edwardahern1860/

Diane Arrelle has more than 350 short stories published and two short story collections: Just A Drop In The Cup and Seasons On The Dark Side. She, her sane husband and insane cat live on the edge of the New Jersey (USA) Pine Barrens (home of the Jersey Devil).

www.arrellewrites.com FaceBook: Diane Arrelle

Dorothy Davies is an editor, writer, photographer and medium. Somehow all these things come together in her seemingly crowded leisure and work life. She is an avid kindle user and delights in writing reviews for Amazon, especially when a novel is deleted a mere 2-3 chapters in and is too badly written to be read… she retired from editing for a while to run a second hand shop, the best one on the Isle of Wight, but the thrill of finding and publishing outstanding stories became too much so she started again with the Gravestone Press imprint. She still runs the shop…

Paul Edwards is a life-long horror fan and writes his own twisted tales in any spare time that he can grab. He has seen three collections of stories published – *Now That I've Lost You* (Screaming Dreams), *Black Mirrors* (Rainfall Books) and *Night Voices* (Demain Publishing), the latter being a joint-collection with author Frank Duffy. Paul is also a fan of role-playing games, rock music and rough Somerset cider.

Jason R Frei lives in Eastern Pennsylvania where he works as a therapist with children and adolescents. He writes speculative fiction culled from the experiences of his life and those he works with and blends science fiction, fantasy and horror into new creations. His flash story "The Garden" will be featured in the horror anthology *99 Tiny Terrors* by Pulse Publishing and his short story "Some of the Parts" will be featured in the horror anthology *Toilet Zone 3: The Royal Flush* by Hellbound Books Publishing. Visit him online: https://facebook.com/odinstones.

Theresa Jacobs entertains readers with her versatile style, from kids' books to horror to crime, she'll never let her creativity be stifled. After writing eleven books in six years, nothing can stop her now. She still works full time in the real world and spends every free moment either writing new stories or binge-watching popular shows. She lives in Canada with her handy husband and goofy dog, both of whom vie for the rest of her time.

Tom Leaf lives in a house with an unpleasant basement, he has no pets, he practices his smile almost every day and has been scrawling words in various notebooks - both lined and unlined - for some years now. Some of his writing makes sense. Thomas is a founding member of the Alcalet Archive and knows that he should be engaging with people on social media whilst developing an effortlessly intriguing bio. He can't right now - he's too busy writing the kind of stories he would like to read.'

Terrance V. Mc Arthur is a storyteller, puppeteer, magician, basket maker and retired librarian, living in the Central Valley of California with his wife, daughter, and the cremains of a cat who lived for 21 years. Terrance's stories have appeared in Thirteen O'Clock Press anthologies.

Brooke MacKenzie is a scary movie fanatic and writes horror fiction by candlelight. Her first book, Ghost Games, will be published later in 2021 by Dreaming Big Publications. She received a B.A. from Sarah Lawrence College and an Ed.M. from the Harvard Graduate School of Education. Her writing has appeared in several places, including Who Knocks? Magazine and The Dead Games: A Zimbell House Anthology. She is the current Board Chair of the New York Writers Coalition, which is the largest community-based writing organization in the country. She lives in Northern California with her husband and daughter. Visit her website: bamackenzie.com

Travis Mushanksi - I was born and raised on the Canadian Prairies where I now work as a professional brewer in the craft beer industry. I graduated from the BA English program at the University of Regina where I focused on creative writing. Over the past ten years, I have worked as a freelance writer and editor for various online projects. I occasionally find myself writing short fiction exploring the nightmares and horrors that hide just out of sight. Of course, all of this is possible because of the support of my wonderful wife, Janelle, and my beautiful daughter, Emma.

Rie Sheridan Rose multitasks. A lot. Her short stories appear in numerous anthologies, including Killing It Softly Vol. 1 & 2, Hides the Dark Tower, Dark Divinations and On Fire. She has authored twelve novels, six poetry chapbooks and lyrics for dozens of songs. She is also editor-in-chief for Mocha Memoirs Press and editor for the Thirteen O' Clock imprint of Horrified Press. She tweets as @RieSheridanRose.

David Turnbull is a member of the Clockhouse London group of genre writers. He writes mainly short fiction and has had numerous short stories published in magazines and anthologies. His stories have previously been featured at Liars League

London events and read at other live events such as Solstice Shorts and Virtual Futures. He was born in Scotland, but now lives in the Catford area of London. He can be found at www.tumsh.co.uk.

Liam A Spinage is a former philosophy student, former archaeology educator and former police clerk who spends most of his spare time on the beach gazing up at the sky and across the sea while his imagination runs riot.

Thomas   M.   Malafarina (www.ThomasMMalafarina.com) has published seven horror novels, as well as seven collections of horror short stories. He has also published a book of often strange single panel cartoons called Yes I Smelled It Too, as well as a Microsoft based technical manual called Link-Tuit. He has written and published more than 200 short stories. All of his horror books have been published through Hellbender Books an imprint of Sunbury Press. (www.Sunburypress.com).